WHAT PEOPLE ARE SAYING ABOUT

DRINK THE REST OF THAT

I've waited years for this book. Guy J. Jackson is a prolific writer of stories that combine dark comedy and tender beauty, populated by extraordinary characters rooted in the ordinary threats of the universe. Imagine if a Kurt Vonnegut/Richard Brautigan hybrid had written *The Phantom Tollbooth* and you are somewhat close to the uniqueness of this book: an old man contemplates existence through the holes in a washing machine; Elton suffers the consequences of living in a house with no clocks; a bank teller whose sideline as a stripper always results in the wrong kind of boyfriends. *Drink The Rest of That* is a dazzling, heartbreaking, laugh-a-loud collection that will leave you wanting more. I'm just hoping there wⁱˡˡ ᵇᵉ ᵃⁿᵒᵗʰᵉʳ 25 ᵛᵒˡᵘᵐᵉˢ

Nathan Penlington – *Choose Your Ou*
The Book

T0159463

Guy J. Jackson's creaking mahogan〉 word of these absurd, dark, delightful, unexpected, abnormal, rich, indulgent, Beefheartean, nightmarish, suburban, Ionescoesque stories, vignettes, and things. He'd be a brilliant babysitter for children who'll never sleep again. "Read me another, Mr. Jackson," they'd cry.

A.F. Harrold – *The Point Of Inconvenience; Harold; Flood*

Reading the stories of Guy J. Jackson is like embracing your long-lost best friend while they play Rachmaninoff 3 with one hand – at once joyous and familiar and extraordinary. Read them in your head on the morning tube and baffle commuters with the knowingness of your smile. Take a pal and a bottle of cheap whiskey to a cove and howl them to the sea. Slip them on like a pair of delicious mind-slippers at nightfall. These are tales for everywhere, for every day, for falling into and in love with again and again.

Gwyneth Herbert – *The Sea Cabinet; All The Ghosts*

In a review of the 2012 album *Notes On Cow Life* for Wire magazine, legendary journalist Byron Coley described Guy's words as 'genial surrealism...probably quite enjoyable when wrecked'. I'm quoting him verbatim as I really couldn't have put it better, and frankly, he carries far more clout than I ever could. I heard Guy's words a long time before I ever saw them written down, that amiable croak of a voice booming tales of the uncanny from stages in cramped rooms above pubs or across the London airwaves on cult radio station Resonance FM. But reading these stories now, I hear that unique voice once again. You'll hear it too.

Robin the Fog – *Secret Songs Of Savamala; The Ghosts Of Bush*

A playful collection brimming with wonderful characters, sharp observations and poignant moments.

Sam Rawlings – *Lazy Gramophone*

A joy to read, lyrical and evocative, subtly disturbing.

Danny Chidgey – *Lazy Gramophone*

Drink the Rest of That

A Short Story Collection

Drink the Rest of That

A Short Story Collection

Guy J. Jackson

Winchester, UK
Washington, USA

First published by Roundfire Books, 2015
Roundfire Books is an imprint of John Hunt Publishing Ltd., Laurel House, Station Approach,
Alresford, Hants, SO24 9JH, UK
office1@jhpbooks.net
www.johnhuntpublishing.com
www.roundfire-books.com

For distributor details and how to order please visit the 'Ordering' section on our website.

Text copyright: Guy J. Jackson 2014

ISBN: 978 1 78279 635 0

A CIP catalogue record for this book is available from the British Library.

Design: Stuart Davies

Printed and bound by CPI Group (UK) Ltd, Croydon, CR0 4YY

We operate a distinctive and ethical publishing philosophy in all
areas of our business, from our global network of authors to
production and worldwide distribution.

CONTENTS

Acknowledgements

Just want to thank Holly, Mom and Dad, Meme, Georgie, Chris, Sean, Clyde, dear friends Clint and Nathan and Pete and Jim and Cliff and Kelly and Kristin and Manny and Toby and Jason and both Chads, teachers Carole Evans and Patricia Hurley, and Stephen King of course, and as well all other kind folks along the way who encouraged or somehow aided and abetted my scribbling. I hope they know who they are, because surprisingly their names are too many for this space.

9 Minutes

An anonymous ski-mask narrator exposing the world's worst public transportation system is what we now have on every channel. You ever hear of *The 9-Minute Rule*? It's the rule whereby if you drop something (like a candy bar) you're about to eat on the ground you have 9 minutes to pick it up and eat it before the germs come. That means your candy bar could be sitting in a puddle of Hepatitis blood and Bovine Spongiform Encephalopathy vomit for 9 full minutes before the germs get to it, and you can stand there staring down at your candy bar in the puddle of blood and vomit for 8 minutes and 55 seconds before picking it up and eating it. Once I knew a fella, though, who dropped his candy bar on bare sidewalk and picked it up 3 seconds later and ate it and still got sick. That's the dilemma of a liberal who found out his dog was a conservative. The guilt of having roasted grasshoppers and watching their hoods turn red. Gotta go to where they doff their shoes before entering. Get the kids obsessed with some little thing or every little thing. Those are also all parts of *The 9-Minute Rule*. Subsets. Clauses.

- The End -

22nd

Old man's brought the dog home, and the old man's rapping our glass front door with his particularly twisted walking stick. Inside, we wait on the sofas, wait for his shouting to begin, tap our toes. Tonight it's only night because the day has failed to pervade a steady rain. Love has reared a typically ugly head, and tomorrow stretches like a fanfare to gum on the streets. No wonder there are cigarettes, you can hardly pick your battles without picking them improperly.

He decided on a rash of anxiety to top off his relaxing weekend in the countryside. A run up and down the library's stone stairs and no sweat on the brow, something stuck in the throat. What was the terrible answer to this the worst of questions? Where does he belong, this spinning spitting sunray of a salmon of a man? The other day in the forest while walking he was approached by a zombie squadron of the old, all of whom had a different question and different waffles to their smiles. He's not quite cut out for this, he's got no eyes for the future. There's those lights away out there, but the sadness is too complete and the burden in the belly too much to burble. Leave home too long and there's no way back. What's the definition of that face down there that windowways, has it got a beard or is it a woman lost in rude shadow?

How could they not want us to take pills and hole up in abstinence and ignore entirely the love of good people when there is so much wrong with every ember, every idyll. You've got your babbling brook, now go back to town and get a boat to put in it my fine-tooled man with your off-putting devices, you filching eyes from our favorite mists, our favorite clocks ticking their favorite times. There's the lights, but they have no comfort, not even the bittersweet brand. Not tonight anyway.

- The End -

70 People Say

My brother had been six months here, and I think never once did he wash his clothes. He was plenty grumpy from never leaving the house and never being close enough to a bathroom. He always thought someday he'd feel different but here he was here, and not only here he was here but here he was here at 97. That's an age, can you believe it? An actual age of a human being. People say: how are you, I know you, very nice to see you. That is, they say that, the ones of us who can carry on a conversation without talking about our long-dead friends or long-dead brothers or sisters or long-dead fathers or mothers. My brother wrote letters to all of them, those lodged in our past, while I begged out of writing letters. I didn't have anything to say to anyone. But even though my brother could write like thunder down the paper he'd absently fold the letters and stuff them in his pockets. I was washing his clothes for him because I had to do something to keep the motors grinding, at least grinding, and I could never remember he stuffed his pockets with letters, so he was finding his letters washed into tattered crumbling wads that fell apart if you tried to unfold them to retrieve the words. "You're not mad at me are you?" I'd ask each time. "They're just words," my brother would say, after saying "WHAT?!" a lot. Then he'd say: "And how am I supposed to send letters to dead people anyhow. You might as well wash them in the washing machine, it's as good a way as any to get the letters into the ether and on their way to the dead people." I wish he hadn't said that. What a thing to say. My brother was six months here, but six months on and I'm still pausing to look into the washing machine for ten-minutes-or-so stretches before the clothes go in. Looking in it for what I don't know. But I used to peer in washing machines as a toddler thinking they went somewhere. And I'm only one year younger than my brother so I'm almost back to being a toddler. So that's what's up. I'm looking for the dimension doors where the letters get posted to the dead people, the doors (or windows) my brother was implying. I'm looking every other day because I'm good about laundry. Yes, I'm looking. Something about those tiny holes.

- The End -

113

113 degree heat today and inside the car feels like a comet. My, that's okay, she's got her substantial lemonade and knickers dragging icicles. I for one haven't been able to lift them, so that counts for icicles. I know I shouldn't say as much. It's the heat piling frustration when I should let it sap frustration and all other strengths.

- The End -

4:30 AM

I don't see how they could hear anything, for example me dragging a chair across the floor or walking about at 4:30 AM with that snoring going down fan-wise down in their apartment, it all stuck in the cracks, the snoring and the chair both.

- The End -

780 Wishes

Once upon a time, she was The Princess Of 780 Wishes. That was down 1,704 wishes from where she had begun. She had also begun as a scullery maid, but she had casually freed a more-than-generous gnome from a well. The gnome wasn't full of trickery, he was grateful for being saved and more than indulgent. When he granted her 2,484 wishes the scullery maid-soon-to-be-princess kept saying: "Are you sure? ... Are you sure? ... Seems like an awful lot of wishes..."

The gnome was sure. He hadn't wanted to die in a well, anything but that. 2,484 wishes was the least he could do.

So the princess was able to save some wishes back.

And some of her wishes had been bad ones. She had wanted to live in the future for example. But after two years of owning her own nightclub, Stiff Upper Lip Neon, in the heart of Los Angeles, she missed the primordial green of pre-history, back when such stuff as scullery maids becoming princesses was only the stuff of the day-to-day, and nobody felt it necessary or even knew how to paint those stories on celluloid.

Our princess hadn't grown accustomed to technology, either, up there in the 1990s, and hadn't known how to leave a decent answering-machine greeting, either, and so if someone called up Stiff Upper Lip Neon they'd hear her dull voice say dully: "Stiff Upper Lip Neon, please leave a message." Her dull voice didn't fit with the idea of answering machines, it just didn't cooperate with the technology and had no business being present with it, and neither did her voice fit the very concept of neon, neon in and of itself. Also, she hadn't come this far into the future, to where you are now reading or hearing of her, dear reader. Because you'd be hard pressed to find an answering machine in anyone's home nowadays, right? She only came as far into the future as to where answering machines had been invented and were in use. She only came up to the 1990s.

But never mind, she went back to her own time. She liked to see blue sky and not smog. She liked to see deer in the fields. She sort of missed indoor plumbing but she could wish for it for herself and she did and then she had indoor plumbing. She didn't understand why humans had invented the car things, the car things which seemed to just not do much besides go from place to place blowing and coughing a poisonous gas. She had enjoyed how far indoor plumbing had come through the ages, but that was about it.

Back in her own time, when she got below one thousand wishes, she spent a couple years counting and worrying. Did she use up wish number such and such yesterday or not? She wished back the gnome teleportation-wise and he didn't mind being interrupted in the middle of dinner with his family at all because the princess was his savior and she asked him if he had kept track of how many wishes she had used and he shrugged and said sorry he hadn't, but he thanked her again for saving him from the well because the backlogged thought of that well still gave him the shudders just to think about, and he then went ahead and topped her up with 545 more wishes. Then the gnome told her how he was so afraid of falling in another well he'd taken to carrying a walking stick and tapping the ground in front of him as he walked. He thought that the stick trick would be good for sightless people to use. He thought, too, that they should build small circular walls to warn him where there were wells.

Then one day the princess wished away her scoundrel

prince and his plotting courtiers, and she wished away death, and found herself sad and alone, but also unworried by anything, even whether the wishes were dwindling stockpile-wise, and she lived happily ever after in her wished-for immortality. *Happily ever after*, by the by, would seem to be just a thing that gets said, and contradictory to 'sad and alone', but it's not.

- The End -

1980

In early June of 1980 I am stopping stressing. Since it's June of 1980 I'm not sure the word has been invented yet. But let me tell you what it means. "STRESS" is an unknown, unseen force inside you that doesn't actually exist but is grinding your mind into powder. You don't want to be stressed because eventually it causes death or at least something like death. Also, death causes death.

In early June of 1980 I rumbled out of San Francisco and went to stay at a friend's house in the Humboldt Hills. His wife had just left him inexplicably. He was the one who used the word 'inexplicably' but once I got there to stay with him I could explain. He lived like there were still peasants in those California hills. He might as well have been an inbred in those California hills, always making toward entropy and never cleaning a dish if he bothered to eat off one and never cleaning his clothes except once a month when he would take them to a nearby stream and dunk them in, ceremoniously, and then hang them to dry from every available tree, no soap involved. It's like when you go hiking with these people who come across caves in the wilderness and say: 'Oh, we could live here'. I didn't mind these habits of my friend and in fact joined in with them but of course his wife must've minded because she had packed up and left him without a word. A clichéd way to leave someone if ever there were. Usually me and women get along okay, but I do feel like his wife could've returned the favor of my friend's apparently undying love and given him one word. At least one.

"Without a word," my friend would say each night in front of the fireplace, uttering the cliché's essence with more gravitas than it deserved, sort of. She could've given him one word so he didn't say that five times a night, every single night. Ten times a night. He'd say that after we'd have an eternal silence between us. Sometimes he stuck out his pinkie and wrote it out on the air while saying it. I read books a lot on those nights, even though books are passé and no one likes them anymore because they smell. I didn't ever reply to my friend saying 'without a word' because it wasn't a question, and mostly I'd be in the middle of some book, and anyway it was only my duty to sit there and be there and mildly field his misery.

Me, I let all my stress drain away, even though this friend of mine was in a hell of his own making because he'd gotten romantically involved with someone else in the world, tsk tsk. But I myself was having a great time imagining what was already imaginary (the stress) drain away from my head like a slow bad hiss of purple steam. I was there in the hills for many months and all through the height of summer. I still smile when I think of those days. You should never feel stress. It doesn't exist. Just like it probably didn't exist in 1980. And in, oh, 1910, they only called it "the flutters".

Eventually I discovered my friend had found a cave even though they were mostly all gone from those California hills. I'd wondered what he was doing with the trees he'd been chopping down in the environs of our cabin and so one day I followed him when he dragged off a tree. He was my friend and I suppose I didn't need to sneak along following him but then again following is always more exciting, stalking in the woods especially, it awakens your sense of what it used to be like back in the day. Nowadays even hunting is passé, and you hear about the few remaining hunters quitting hunting all the time because they have to get drunk to do the actual act of hunting and then they're just drunk and hanging around the woods forever waiting for a moose and sometimes they're drunk enough to shoot one another and finally the hunters give it up forever and tell everyone how hunting is actually totally boring and then they go to an exercise resort to get rid of their beer guts.

When I followed my friend I found he'd found a cave and built an elaborate door frame and door for the entrance. He was just putting the finishing touches on when I got there, using the last tree for a hitching post outside the door. For a horse, I guess, though he didn't own a horse but maybe his visitors would or maybe he was getting one later instead of a car. Reverse flow. Not me, though. I mean I suppose I was one of his visitors but I don't own a horse because horses never seemed to me like they should be owned. Nobody ever asked horses if they wanted anyone sitting on their backs. Imagine if we've all been riding horses for thousands of years by mistake! But point being: others of his visitors. I watched my friend from a stand of aspen as he planted his hitching post in a posthole and then de-barked it, which I thought he could've done the opposite way around. I sat there in the aspen thinking about how he was probably doing what he was doing the wrong way around but I didn't want to go talk to him about it, it wasn't my place, it was only my place to watch right then. I thought about my mom once telling me how aspens, or anyway ONE aspen, was respon-sible for the largest tree in the world. I thought about how with the door on it so that you could close it shut, my friend's cave he'd found was going to be so much darker.

- The End -

A Cabin with No Fireplace

Elton lived in a cabin with no fireplace. He still knew heat from the bars of his space heater and the scratchy blankets on his bed, and he still knew comfort from the overlarge sweaters he wore, but he just wasn't so sure that any feelings of warmth came out truthfully from his heart.

In the woods surrounding the cabin lived The Pokatee. At night, Elton carved quacking ducks from bars of soap while he squinted out at The Pokatee's blue-tinged campfires. During the day, when Elton glimpsed The Pokatee, they were slinking in among the trees in their costumes of wood and plaster and the amber lights of their eyes were all that showed of their faces and all that showed of the rest of The Pokatee was their enormous hands with just three fingers that looked coated in spider fur and flickered like snakes. It made Elton somewhat uncomfortable to be the only human living in the midst of what was obviously the part of the forest belonging to The Pokatee.

Elton never liked to think he even had any core of emotion, but sometimes broken ptarmigan would crash land in the woods surrounding the cabin and Elton would have to rescue the ptarmigan from the hunger of The Pokatee. As long as Elton walked out from his cold cabin with a fist-sized stone that he tossed in the air and caught one-handed The Pokatee would leave him alone. Elton would walk out and scoop up whichever stunned ptarmigan while The Pokatee, hidden behind nearby trees, made a ruckus sharpening their dinner knives.

But then the ptarmigan always half-flew, half-hopped away to unknown fates just a few nights from Elton taking them in, and Elton knew it was because the ptarmigan could eat seeds from the false-pewter bowl of seeds Elton put out for them, and the ptarmigan could preen their feathers on the hewn legs of Elton's one-and-only table, but they could never ever warm their ruffs by sitting near the blank cabin wall.

"A good load of bricks," said Elton, as he sat in the evenings and carved soap ducks and kept an eye on The Pokatee and mused on what he figured was the first step in getting the ptarmigan to stay.

- The End -

A Freeway in the Clouds

Bespectacled Chad Danvers is there now, driving his Ford pickup along the 280. It's sunny out. Chad likes how they add diamonds to the asphalt when they make the roads. There's a small monkey in the passenger seat attempting to and failing to play an ukulele. Chad's not sure if the monkey is real. If the monkey is real, it sure doesn't like to do much besides fail to play that fucking ukulele. If the monkey is a toy, Chad wishes its batteries would run out.

Coming up alongside Chad's Ford is a sea-blue car, with a frizzy-haired girl driving. Chad likes frizzy-haired girls. When seeing them on the freeway he always pulls his time-travel trick. He pulls it now. He FOCUSES, focuses light against speed, and him and the frizzy-haired girl time travel back to the year 1864, and the road is suddenly made of dirt, and they are both suddenly driving horse-drawn wagons. So now Chad is able to shout to the frizzy-haired girl, and she can hear him.

"Hi!" Chad shouts. But she's no different than all the other frizzy-haired girls. She panics at the sudden time travel. She screams and holds her head as though her mind is going to blow. The horses pulling her wagon react badly to her screams and break off in a wild gallop, leaving Chad's wagon far behind, in a cloud of choking dust. Chad coughs and says: "Aw, man." Then he FOCUSES, focuses light versus velocity, and sends both himself and the frizzy-haired girl back to the present day. Up ahead and in her car once more the frizzy-haired girl slams on the brakes and pulls over to the side of the road. Chad slows and drives by and sees she's okay, though gripping the steering wheel and dumping hysterical tears. So Chad drives on, shaking his head and saying aloud to himself: "Man, you always fuck things up with that time-travel bullshit."

The monkey with the ukelele apparently agrees, because it reinvigorates its strumming of the ukelele and sings in a human voice:

Chad Chad Chad
always fucking things up
with his time-travel bullshit
ooo ooo ooo
Chad Chad Chad
always fucking things up
with his time travel bullshit
ooo ooo ooo

Hmmm, thinks Chad. *Must be a real monkey after all.*

- The End -

A Good Dream

He ducked his headful of knitted hair under the Ardindron Crossbeam wherewith he usually hit his head and then he was down at the drain of the stairs the first floor of the cabin the walls of which were not exactly there in the dark the night scene of which was crickets and hollow air but it was only that a nonsense song had woken him up skittering around in his head singing a way down through Miss Mynwyn's door you kiss the child's bedroom floor and the coats were whispering on the coat rack and so somehow with those things he was sure his dead daughter was outside as he felt her as a hunch and through their shared blood even if her blood was nowadays streamed into ghostliness as he padded across the carpet so worn it didn't much matter but at least it wasn't as cool as bare wood and when he opened the front door or maybe it was opened for him there was indeed something of a teenage girl down by the lake while written on the porch in letters that blazed yellow for a moment and then snuffed and scattered out into the dark were the words *blue truck* while the sky had out every one of the stars and the moon was a scythe that in his blurred vision sliced half that sky and under it he strode out not even taking the stop to slip on his thongs watching that he didn't step on any baby Crosscarriane Frogs on the way to the lake as the frogs were out in harmless millions this spring along the lakeside hatching alongside where his dead daughter was standing out in the water tangled with the reeds glowing and smeared in her form him saying to her as he arrived nearby *I miss you* as she glanced at him over one half-shoulder breathed a saucer of light his way then evaporated as he awoke with a light heart and tears on his temples and looked up into the cabin rafters and marveled at how silent and still they played it while his wife was gone from the bed and he could whiff she was downstairs making bacon and eggs. "That was a good dream," he said to himself.

- The End -

A House with No Clocks

Elton lived in a house with no clocks. He still saw the sun and he still saw the moon and he still always knew sort of what hour it was, but he knew no precision in time.

On Elton's neighbor's lot, Elton's neighbor had never built a house, and lived in just a trailer peppered with bullet holes. The neighbor scared Elton. The neighbor always wore a dirty skycap, and he was made like a tree. He looked like he could beat Elton up, and Elton didn't want to get beaten up anymore.

Sometimes tame seagulls would amble by on the beach. Elton was afraid of the seagulls laughing at him and never made any effort to scold them from his property. Elton's neighbor never scolded the seagulls from his section of beach, either, and would in fact lurch down the stretch of sand and greet and somehow invite the seagulls back up to and inside the trailer. Elton watched these goings-on from his upstairs window with tears dripping off his cheeks.

Then Elton would turn from the window, and hunch over his model train set, and he would try and guess, in pure desperation, for the very life of him, the exact minute the model train would arrive in the model station and unload its cargo of sugar cubes.

- The End -

A Single Corner

They called the bike trail The Path To Certain Eternity, spelt like that, with four Ts, and thereby no one knew whether the bike trail could make them better. Along it rides myself, an overweight slushpile drifting between absolute power and absolute decay. I can't decide which but the trail pulls me further into the trees and along between painted white lines. At times I want to stop and get to know a single corner of the universes they have here, this spack of paint or this bench. I speak directly to God (but don't follow me for that): "Additional reasons you should take me up into your bosom immediately: I am tough, I require almost no maintenance, it is to parody understatement to say I love and I have life." I peddle sometimes. If only it wasn't for the fence I could go down and swim in that lake, but there's something about the fence even though this isn't America. Mid-'70s music, the singers all dead, jounces from a box taped somewhat to my handlebars. I pass by the same schizophrenic man out there walking and holding his head, every day that man, he must be a former child star, the handsomeness, the white hair. I will come upon that man, that man with his fingers laced schizophrenically in the fence, laced in the chain link, and the man yelling at the sky. I want to approach the man, but it's none of my business. Funny how you can sniff schizophrenia off the way someone laces their fingers in chain link. They don't even have to yell at the sky, you can just suss them by them lacing their fingers in chain link in schizophrenic fashion. I can't go home with these visions in my head if I don't approach the man someday soon, or promise myself to approach him. That was just childhood, I'll say. At least you were a spoiled brat on the set of a popular family TV show with craft service etcetera instead of getting beat up by Denny Wentworth in the locker room, I'll say. You shouldn't read too much into childhood, I'll point out. I can't go home without promising myself absolutely and unquestionably that next time I come this way again I'll approach the man and make him better for tomorrow. I'm too shy now. And I have to go home and listen to the one favorite song of my neighbor that my neighbor plays at top volume over and over and over again, because I guess my neighbor never tires of those lyrics about me being more than a man to you and you being more than a woman to me and you being not just my lover and me being not just your friend.

- The End -

Able Table

Ain't that the way, you turn up and talk to the black and white dog behind the bar and he's too shy. Or she, whatever. You spend more time talking to the bartender's dog than the bartender, and it's hard to slight a bartender but the bartender is slighted by that, believe you me. No matter what kind of triumph you have winning a new car or whatever you turn around and slight the bartender and your day isn't perfect. No matter what kind of shattering depression you have over your morbidly obese mother or whatever you can still ruin your day still moreso by slighting the bartender. And the dog doesn't listen. He only knows 100 words, and those words will only be English words depending on his owner. Anyhow, me, that next day, I'd just encountered stinging nettles for the first time and now I had to sit at my table and drink and then go home for able bits of sleep. Then along came the Pickle Ship. It was a food concoction that cured general itchiness and it was made of pickles and bread and sardines and sunflower oil and garlic dressing and tasted amazingly surprisingly good. I discovered it in the pub, then made one for myself for breakfast every morning from then on, and came upon new lands of food energy, which I exploit to this day, in order to get my digital desk duties done.

- The End -

ACTPA

Acknowledge Clarify Test Propose Agree is what someone once taught me to think against the word "NO". But I was never quick enough. Did you know there were still salesmen in this country? I didn't know that. What would a salesman sell? Hasn't everything been sold? Aren't we by now programmed to buy? Other people have told me that when I pretend at salesmanship my smile 'unfurls', and I like the sound of an unfurling smile. Other people have told me that when I pretend at sales I 'detail' things, like I detail shops that I'm about to rob, and I like to hear that too.

Eating paper is just as good as alcoholism, did you know?

Pick up your cell phone and say I lv u once in awhile.

I am the 55% and I say the 45% can go jump in a lake. How convenient that I'm in the 55%. I guess that means I'm in the majority. The majority. Delightful. How perfect that I'm in the majority.

Alcohol is a fact. It's a fact.

I keep meaning to persecute bacon but I never get around to it.

Or how about The Ol' Talking Over The Wind Trick? Eh? You ever try that? Talking Over The Wind or better yet Screaming Over The Wind? I mean especially when someone is teaching you the principles of ACTPA in an airless office with a foam ceiling and florescent light and no air and the door goes WHOOSH when it shuts because no air and the blinds come down during the day and there's only one window and you can't get out even though you can see out the window to the river and the ducks and the rocks you used to climb without the extra pounds and the booze sloshing around in your legs.

Gee. Maybe they're just teaching me this stuff so they don't have to talk me down when I've climbed to the top of an old unused telephone pole. But even thinking that I start thinking how we all miss telephones.

- The End -

Actress

The makeup always stuck to her eyelashes. The hope always stuck to the roof of her mouth. The dreams always crumbling, and as far-fetched as possible. Margie Triple, and her career as an actress. She gets the idea in her head that she really oughtta audition for a school play, and when she does she discovers she's a natural show-off. She would always be starring in an infinite movie that she made up as she went along as a kid in the car with her mom chauffeuring her to and from the video store for still more movies. Sometimes there'd be so many movies she'd get in trouble for sneaking away to rent one, the same as her sneaking away to get alcohol. Scampering through nighttime and the snow for what? *Oil Man*. A dull movie, but her grandmother taught her to sit through dull movies by taking her to *Julia in Gold* three times as a child. She stood outside the pinball arcade in the warm California air and her grandmother and great aunt decided on another viewing of *Julia in Gold* without Margie having any say-so. Can they see in? Margie would wonder, when she was getting out of the shower and toweling off and noticing that she'd left the blinds a hair more open than she would've liked to have had before getting in the shower. And that all the way to today, when she found *Wings of My Friends* so silly. How movies just went on and on. The more you got to subsisting on movies the more tangled you could be about it. Her grandmother's memories of movies, when her grandmother died at 93 and loved the movies since being a child? Phew. So Margie acted in movies in the mirror. Or then she'd volunteered to sport the costume of the school mascot. Stood on the sidelines with the harridan girls from Farwell and Glacier screaming insults at her, then suddenly she'd capered. But the first play was very early, *Hansel and Gretel*. The girls from Hamilton building the wooden cage for Hansel. Just the one line had been tough. She'd waited in flat blocking to shout it out. And Margie was worried about getting old. Shit, it would be just the same as childhood. Now she was using up the candle she'd bought her boyfriend. Selfish, like all those who belong on the stage. If only she could guide her entire life with Derrill Phils as a constant soundtrack. Like guiding a snake to swallow its tail. She'd walked the university stage late at night, staying up and bouncing rubber balls off the walls to help memorize lines. Caught by a security guard, back in the days when campus security didn't care. She'd been so hard on campus security. When she didn't have a place to live she slept in amongst the props in the basement, but the professors had quickly shut down that dream. Then she'd gone to sleep with Terrance, like every other good girl. Heroin at 27, deep in the wilds of L.A. A boyfriend who preferred cocaine. Hanging out with bad actresses, or actresses who had 'made it' for no good reason, or pop stars. She'd find a lot of her hair in the sink. She'd stand in the mirror and spend an hour putting on lipstick. She'd walk the beach and watch the paparazzi descend on one then another then another of her fellow beachgoers. The paparazzi could never catch her. Why, in Santa Barbara she walked from Cabrillo Beach to Henry's Beach without getting killed by the tide. Eventually she could just outwalk the paparazzi, if they ever decided to pursue her. She thought acting was a noble cause. Not only did actors have to be at the mercy of casting directors, at the mercy of what writers would write for them, then at the mercy of the directors themselves, the actors also lay at the mercy of what the studio did with a film. That was a fuck of a lot of mercy to give up and let go. So much of her work wound up in bargain bins at video stores. Then all the video stores closed down. She'd visited her mom in Oregon and lo, they'd found one of her movies in someone's garage sale. But at least she wasn't one of those planning a bombing run on some Middle Eastern village or t'other. She pointed out to everyone who'd listen that she could as well be in an office pushing money around or she could be in a war room planning a bombing run or she could even be selling food she knew was bad for the eaters of it, but she wasn't, she was just out there on the stage or on film trying to hold the mirror up to humanity in her little way. So fuck it if there was no money involved. She even went to Greece, and stood in their ruined amphitheaters, thinking about pregnant women miscarrying when the Furies came rushing out. She doubted she'd ever get pregnant. She could just feel deep within her that she'd never get pregnant. She could go riding mopeds with olive-skinned boys with aplomb, thanks. She'd wanted to get in on that French theatre in Marseilles, poked around out there, and then she'd forgotten it with the drinking she did on the Riviera. Those times. She pointed out how everyone at least once in their life has seen a movie or a play that affected them deeply. She pointed out how humanity without art would be either wandering the planet slapping their heads in confusion or drones about everything including sex. Old recorders, that she'd sing into, that she'd tell rambling narratives into. She wondered how she'd ramble when she got old. A steady stream of dialogue from plays she'd hoped for roles in. The parrot of the old folks' home. How long it used to take to write a thousand words in her acting journal that she'd started in class so very long ago. Nowadays a thousand words was a breeze. She rattled through yellow legal pads like a hedgehog in dead leaves. If only she hadn't lost her very dear friend's vanity-published *Guide to Acting* then everything would have been much more perfect.

- The End -

Acts of Laziness

You can change the world with the laziness of not buying a new car. I stepped on a blanket. Holds no secret no cloud should hold. They disapprove of liquor and yet they sell liquor. He stumbled through the war agog at all the fireworks. Your housekeeper began to love your bulldog. Chartreuse is a blend of green and yellow. They're all there agreeing what a bad person I am. Crushed poppy seeds with the base of the coffee cup. What do you say to a celebrity in a coffee shop? Soon we'll be the minority soon, so please stop bullying them. In here before with baby eyes puffed. The un-criminal element allowed him to stay an entire box of coffee filters. She sat across from him bored while he tried his hand at various all-you-eat contests. GARAGE SALE FOR BRAIN TUMOR CURE said the sign. When the palm trees burned they sent the old men firemen. Firefighting, there's a case for the old. Canal turning into a can of sausages. And that's meant to be funny.

- The End -

Addendum to Notes on the Red Truck

Grew new perspective amidst the horns on my head and went to wait in the farthest end of the tundra clockwise from the Mackinnon Mine.

Never did I see something so lonely.

I suppose they'd expanded the bed and never thought to leave room for love in technology.

I'd rather wait and watch here in the rain at this end of the tundra, the farthest end, here by the Mackinnon Mine, wait for her to come back to my bed even though the bed rattles with its digital design, and I'd rather wait and watch here in the rain for the sun is false the way it makes you feel affirmed.

These doings out in the country. You hear now about some friend of the farmer's, so-called friend who took the farmer's unfriendliest barely born puppy of the litter, thought he was being friendly to the farmer by nurturing the runt, letting the runt as it grew ride in the front of the canoe.

What they get up to my neighbors, and what they must think of me stepping out on the tundra as best I can again and again. Who are they these days? Not that I know my neighbors, y'see. But who do they think they are and does this peace drive them mad?

- The End -

ADULTMART

ADULTMART is a shop for adults where they can buy all sorts of plastic things to put in places.

I'll tell you what: being a Buddhist is the least expensive way to be.

Regard them, these sleepy outposts rolling by, each with their one ADULTMART neon sign.

Wonder: could these neon signs be the only prides of these places?

We're all the same as the plastics, we're all scattered across the land until there's some of us all over. We're in a mysterious row of non-descript houses and this is us. We're in a stand of aligned, hand-planted trees and this is us. We're outside a bar smoking and this is us. We're on a roof amongst the twirling windmills brand new to the roof and this is us.

I got off the train in Tulatin, home of ADULTMART, capitol city of ADULTMART. Dropped my wallet, couldn't find it, had to get back on the train. Someone in Tulatin has my wallet, and is pretending to be me, even though Tulatin is a small town and everyone there knows that someone both as me and as who they were before they found my wallet.

These porters are hardcore that work the train, they are still moving when they get off after their many days of rocking and they have no interest in making transitory friends with the wayward.

You ever wonder what they got around back of the ADULTMART warehouse, living in the palettes? It's an elf. Not plastic. Not ceramic. An elf. Not magic. Not immortal. But an elf. Pointy-eared albino with a bow and arrow for his food. No joke. I heard them saying. Well what? You have to have at least one elf, living in at least one place, or else what's this paradise worth anyway?

I kept showering in these train station shower rooms with these flip flops I had and I'd miss the train going on and I'd have to wait a day to catch the next train. You'd think you wouldn't want a day wasted with the cure for cancer in your hip pocket.

But those at ADULTMART, we can't stop worrying for those, those that insist The Land Of Opportunity somehow means The Land Of Pleasure.

- The End -

Adventure Eve

I woke up at midnight with my head stuffed in amongst some couch pillows. I stepped on the floor and found my feet in heels. Some rascal. I held my head. I took off the heels, surprised I knew how to do it like a professional woman. I thought over how I should spellbind the audience much more. I went to the mirror. I asked several questions I already knew the answer to. She came up beside me. "You've got some writing you're doing," she said. I nodded. "But you can't write your own story," she said. Such hadn't occurred to me. Her voice was shrill so I moved back from the mirror and left her and went down the hall toward a candlelit room at the end. All of this was unfamiliar. I hadn't been in the house, I hadn't met the girl. I wondered if I was free to wander. I didn't reach the room at the end of the hall and instead turned left and found a discussion going on about the protests of the war. That horror that loomed in our periphery. They kept saying it was winnable but it was lost with the death of the first infant, by the way. Incorporating things necessary to memory I thought briefly of breakfast then scolded myself for thinking so small. I talked quickly toward how they were young. I twitched my eyebrow in a half-frown as to what might be happening in the kitchen. I thought of a thousand monkeys and how every once in awhile I might write a good sentence. I was just practicing. How if one book could be. How when I was young and didn't mind my shoes wherever they were discarded. Much better the new perch, the legs stretched out into the current. Perhaps in the airplane over the ocean and they captured their own tail. So what I was really looking for was safety, and then contentment. The nominal findings of my own architecture were that I could build anything anywhere and convince folks to have any amount of homesteading. Yoga seems to me a good add as soon as possible. I stand in the room at the end with the kids all ten years younger talking and grinning at my old smell. I should've kept the heels. That would've entertained them. Spellbound them for a minute.

- The End -

Adventures in the Forbidden Zone

You hunt up a brick. You don't just find a brick on a suburban street. You'd think they would just be there. You'd think of bricks as common. But most homes are cheap these days, they aren't made out of brick and there's not just bricks lying around. Not like there used to be. You'd think people would keep bricks in their yards by the garage door, just for casual use. For holding tarps down. For crushing spiders. For holding cars without brakes in place. But bricks are actually sometimes hard to come by. You find yourself sneaking around the sides of houses looking for them. Bricks are hard to come by and so are stones perfectly-sized. But what you want is a brick, so never mind the stones. You got to eventually break a piece off someone's garden wall to get a brick. Bricks are perfect and that's why they're cliché to our purpose, but they're perfect and so they're desirable clichés. But you mustn't throw too hard, you'll throw out your arm. That is to say, you mustn't do that throwing too hard to throw out your arm when you throw the brick you finally find at the bottom of someone's rainspout. No, no. That was two broken thoughts. Collect into one thought. Okay. You mustn't throw out your arm when you throw the brick through your ex-girlfriend's and/or ex-boyfriend's window.

- The End -

Advising

Advising the English lady to drink a bottle of wine was okay. Advising the American lady to drink a bottle of wine was NOT okay.

Their clothes bore a frequency of food stains, varying in color and spread, from all the cuisines they'd gone through throughout Paris and New York.

The French prostitute spits between her teeth. You can follow her trail of spit spots backward to where Casper Alvea is looking for you. Or to where she started the night from. Whichever comes first. That was the prostitute devising a theory of advising her fellow French people against bottles of wine, if you can believe that.

The dining car liked to rumble against the tracks. Against the people across from you in the dining car you brace against the wind of their politics. They're so angry to be eating with you. Why did you bring up health care? And then you offering that bottle of wine to the American lady? NOT okay. A bottle of wine with breakfast does not go down in America the same as it does in other countries. Against the rails, against the fierce look of the tattooed arm-pumper as he dips angrily into his omelet. Hey, I wasn't hitting on her, buddy, you're right there and I got a wife, too, she's right here, it was just a harmless invitation to alcoholism. Oh, maybe that's it. Maybe they aren't down with it. And now my opinions about health care are confirmed for them, they think me moot against my drinking, and I drink away the day and they think my health-care ideas moot.

Casper Alvea is looking for you. He has the ostensible bottle-of-wine gift but knowing Casper and yours' past he might first present the wine bottle as a gift and then hit you over the head with it.

Advice: Don't Drink With Casper.

The sun in the car, it's relentless. This meal is relentless. How did Amtrak ever come up with the idea of forcing complete strangers across from each other and the forced conversation when you don't want to talk to anyone when you're drunk for breakfast? Why do I want to talk to anyone set in my ways against these rails and against this train and against this landscape, when I have my own thoughts and am so settled in my ways. Drink my way across seven states until my clothes bear a frequency of food stains, and I'm outside my clothes, until it's their clothes, hers and his, bearing a frequent food stain always the same color brown.

But she did look at her husband, plaintive; she wanted to have a drink with me.

- The End -

Afforded Them

Trapped in his own home Norby once upon a time arrested for drugs and almost two weeks in juvie would devise endless Games Of Watchfulness to keep himself occupied these Games in all without beginning middle end when he was under house arrest, ol' Norby, with an ankle bracelet that beeped a warning when he went so far down the lawn back when the city had tried to save money by not putting teens in jail before a coffee-making corporation later came along to give the city money for putting teens in House Jail but each ankle bracelet cost a quarter of a million dollars but the gorgeous Mayor Amy'd afforded them by cutting funding for everything else and these Games Norby often won stuck indoors with thoughts that turned to Games for example he'd Watch The Rays Of Sunrise Gruff Past The Dog's Water Bowl and Norby'd then throw out hows for how long the stuff made of sunrise took to wander past the water bowl and also too there was The Dice Game because there was no television allowed and somehow they knew when the cable guy came and boy Norby can tell you it's no fun to sit home and watch television anyhow once you know you have to sit home and watch television and also books were out by the way because Norby thought books were stupider than television and he always wanted to live in the past 30 years before television so he could yell at a kid he would have about getting off the couch and away from that book and outside to play and anyway Norby halfway down the lawn testing the beep of the ankle device then all the rest of the day The Game called Watching A Beetle Make Its Way Stalk To Stalk To Stalk To Stalk To Stalk Of Grass Going To Wherever and this beetle just across The Line Of Demarcation just over there on the other side of "The Maginot Line" just over there on the other side of "The Mariana Trench" (*ha ha* thought Norby as he thought *The Maginot Line cracks me up every time*) there just the beetle free but not Norby because of his drug use and his House Jail and by the way by the way by the way the house arrest arresters forgot to check the house Norby was arrested in for drugs when they arrested him in it so he was doing FINE watching sunbeams full of stuff thank you watching beetles doing fine in The Games like an Olympiad in his case because the daylight fog came down and why not daylight fog when you missed your friend gone these many years the way Norby missed him gone these many years and tell you what folks you have not lived until you've seen daylight as fog it's a most enterprising sight and most enterprising of daylight a thing to do for itself but now what Norby needs come to think of it is for the sun to go down behind clouds and for a cold front and for actual fog to be collecting on the eaves because The Fog Watching Game that would be !!!SOME KINDA GAME!!! and so Norby finds himself as he finds himself in vain so often these days he finds himself in vain as he wishes in vain for The Fog Watching Game here in Fresno.

- The End -

After 57 Days

After 57 days inside his house, which was in turn inside his bio-dome, which was in turn upon his moon, Arthur emerged from the house into the electric brick-walled backyard. When he opened the door the yellow dog spilled out. The yellow dog immediately trotted over to a filthy digital tennis ball lying toward the middle of the emerald lawn, and scooped the ball into its mouth. While Arthur was good about letting the yellow dog into the backyard to poop and pee, Arthur had not, for the last 57 days, come out his own self. But now there Arthur stood, blinking at the sunlight that smashed across the surface of the bio-dome, twitching his ears against the murmurs of the signal towers, stretching, licking microchips from his fingertips. So the yellow dog was presuming that Arthur might want to play.

Arthur spoke his thoughts aloud, per his custom. "Well. I'm out. And it's still all evil I see."

Arthur looked to the deep dark of space that icily ensconced the sun.

"Evil," he said.

Arthur looked to the lavender linoleum trees. "Still evil," he said.

Arthur looked to the yellow dog. "You're not evil. But. You are either hosting an evil parasite or incubating an evil life form from another moon besides our own. Whatever the case, it only needs a catalyst, and it will take you, yellow dog."

The yellow dog grinned around the ball in its mouth. Arthur sternly shook his head. The yellow dog wagged its tail. Arthur drew in breath. The yellow dog dropped the ball to the grass, in a tease.

"Ah," said Arthur, and he, too, let go a smile, the smile an alien zipper that didn't belong on Arthur's face, so similar as his face was to the surface of his worthless moon.

Arthur advanced, testing each bare foot in the stilettos of emeralds that passed for grass.

"Ow," said Arthur.

"Shoes," said Arthur.

But he made it to the tennis ball. He saw himself in the future, perched on a shut toilet and scouring the bottoms of his feet for thin cuts from this evil, gem-planted lawn of his. Too kept. He imagined reprogramming the robot gardener so he could teach the lawn a lesson.

Arthur picked up the ball and threw it. The yellow dog gave chase. The ball bounced sparks off a section of brick path lit from within, then evaporated into a denim hedgerow.

The yellow dog went in after and also vanished.

A long period passed.

Arthur listened uselessly for any life beyond his own. Arthur listened to clouds of condensation form and burn away inside the bio-dome's upper reaches. He listened to the one true evil, the eye of the Demon itself, the sun, scratching its way across a few million billion miles of hopelessly cold space.

"Hey?! Yellow dog?!" Arthur called out.

Nothing.

Finally, Arthur minced forward, stepping from the unbearable pain of the grass to the intolerable heat of the bricks. He reached the hedgerow, peered through. The yellow dog was lying on its side in the loam beyond, its chest pumping too quick for breathing. Three-inch-long metallic blue beetles had swarmed from its mouth. The beetles spewed oily, gluey fluid from their own mouths, working toward enshrouding the dog's body in a cocoon that shimmered with the oblivion of the bottom of the ocean.

Arthur stepped back from the hedge. He headed for the house, lickety-split. His feet were going like pancakes on the bricks.

"Shoes!" he said.

Once back inside, in the gloom and safety, Arthur drifted through the labyrinth of computers on computers on monitors on monitors, the flashing lights, the blinking buttons. He tripped to the couch but didn't fall over the cables so numerous they hid the floor in a humming jungle. He flopped down among nylon pillows, pulled a pile of foil blankets over himself, and most especially over his head. He became still. He stared into the pattern of the couch. A universe of black and white checks. He breathed.

"Arthur," he said, scolding, but gently, gently, so as not to rile his own innards. "Arthur? Is there really any reason to go out? You didn't need to go out for the past 57 days. Why today? Learn your lesson. Learn your lesson..."

He closed his eyes. He spun.

- The End -

Ale

The ale ate at him with a fine cramp. He never could kick anything out of his mind that bothered him greatly, but he certainly forgot all good things that happened. The new fine friend, the giraffe. It lay out in the living room like mother's rug. "Momma, I'm so sorry," he cried with one corner of one frosty eye. He wrote notes he never sent to her, kitchen letters, and he always adored the way ink spilled into the paper to create words but he never cared for the words, which couldn't ever express the depths of his thankfulness for being alive. Yawns came along like pleasant interruptions. They advised him of the curb after he'd already tumbled from it. He paused in a darkly lit stair, and tapped his cigarette. The bus whirled through the night and he woke up at a rest area in a food plaza. He didn't know what rest areas were called by the British. There was a truckload of chickens there, though, and one of the bunch of chickens was actually really whistling. A little precursor to his later veganism life choices. Later he met himself as a kid and told of the sights of age 60 to himself, and the kid said "Wow." Later he thought of The Wall as sitting and suffering for China itself. Later still he fell suddenly in love and dropped the decorating he was doing in the shop window and ran out to the sidewalk and scooped up the lady's terrier and unhooked the terrier from its leash and then ran, ran for it, running as hard as he'd ever run, through the city streets and all the way to the edge of the city, running through just a patch of suburbs before running into the country, the terrier enjoying the ride, lying still and jouncing like a baby in his arms, and they ran together until they found a wooded glen, an abandoned cabin they fixed up together, him fixing and the terrier observing, kibitzing with barks, fixing up the cabin until it had even throw rugs like Momma's and a long human bed for him and a round bed for the terrier, and a warm fire in the fireplace each cozy night. But this was all the future, and right now was the past, and the ale shuffling around liver-ways.

- The End -

All Hell

I'm inventing a clever ratchet set and the wife has allowed me to quit my job and stay home to titter over it but as such now that she leaves for her own job each morning all hell breaks loose with the dog discovered to be peeing on the rug all this time and also he buries in the apartment floor six-packs of CK Malt Liquor and ramen bundles that I find.

Why would my dog do that to me?

Tittering over my clever ratchet set that I'm inventing because I don't want to laugh too loud like a scientist, mind you. Every morning I don't laugh too loud, I keep it in check.

They're only ratchets after all, though they're clever.

I try to keep my tread light, too, hereabouts; we have the apartment above these days.

Used to be the apartment below, and we'd never once hear the people above so I keep my tread light because I know I can be heavy. And heavy-lidded, ha ha. Used to be the apartment below with mildew scattering the walls and my wife's asthma climbing and my wife not having a job. But now at least our apartment has risen.

These days, below, you can hear the snores of our below neighbor, powerful snoring filtering up through the floor in not-so-much tendrils but something like tendrils but that would be appropriate for the size of the neighbor's snores. A word I don't have handy but it's somewhere in my ratchet set. But I don't know from ratchets. My Uncle Marilyn does though, he likes motorcycles much to my chagrin. You go into his apartment and you'll see motorcycles climbing the walls when you sit at the very comfortable wet bar my Uncle Marilyn built out of car seats and drink one of his very comfortable 7&7s. I'm nervous for my Uncle Marilyn about how they say it's only a matter of time before you fall down on a motorcycle and how serious or not serious the crash winds up being.

My wife goes off to her job and I discover the dog has formulated an incredible pee stain beneath the living room rug, like an articulate cloud, like if the floor was made of wood which it is, and the floor became dark instead of light, which it did. I'm not usually one to talk of such things. Usually I lie very cleanly.

On Saturday I cycled to La Mirada to meet a girl about a wrench. The ride was very pleasant because I think someone at the bicycle shop had taped a pint of vodka under my bicycle seat which I was surprised to find. Unlike my Uncle Marilyn I do not ride an electrical and gas-powered machine but a bicycle that only needs a bit of lubricant now and then. La Mirada is known as "a place where water appears and then disappears so you thought it was there" in Spanish but in English it's known mysteriously as La Mirada. It was a four-hour bicycle ride but I needed the exercise because of what happened last year between me and alcohol and ramen noodles. No, in answer to your question, I don't know what's so delicious about noodles, and I don't understand the appeal. Ancient genetic programming about stuffing ropy things in your mouth, I suppose, from back in ancient pagan times which went on for bajillions of years of stuffing the mouth with ropy things. Ha! That one goes out to you, Andy.

I'm surprised you didn't ask about why I'd cycle four hours for a simple wrench. But apparently, according to the advertisement in the nickel paper I'd found wedged between two washing machines when I was washing the dog's bed which he'd also peed in, it was a special wrench. Of the type made by the Sears company before they went out of business and their parking lots became windblown wastelands of dirty blowing plastic bags. Sears had, in 1975, cornered the market with their series of wrenches hand-designed by Brooks Badnor, a German (of course) who'd studied his wrenches to match the average white male arm. Yes, okay, so they were racist wrenches, but I'm not a racist. Hey, look, the Volkswagens you see people driving around were designed by Hitler to transport Aryans specifically and no one comments on that. Why shouldn't I take advantage of a wrench designed specifically to the pale, whispery, crumbling, reedy failings of my tired white arm? And anyway, the wrench wasn't even for me, if you must know, it was intended for my Uncle Marilyn, who has the same lilywhite arm as I do, and I want him to have a good wrench specifically so he gets his bolts tight and doesn't crash his motorcycle. Listen, speaking of uncles, I have two mulatto cousins and nine African-American second cousins and five African-American sets of aunts and uncles once removed all because of my aunt and uncle interracially marrying, so I'm the furthest thing from racist. Look, you don't tell IBM that you don't want their Aryan nation calculators even though those IBM people came specifically out of Hitler's meetings to build computers that worked only for blondes with blue eyes. Which is why for example Taylor Swift is a famous-these-days-blonde-and-blue-eyed computer programmer who does very well with computers.

Isn't it convenient how I can just say HITLER and you know exactly who I'm talking about? They should change his name to just the one name, to follow suit behind LIZA, who's this old-timey queen they had on the radio back when speaking for her husband who couldn't talk into microphones because he was ch-ch-ch-chickenshit.

I heard this Christian girl in La Mirada had one of these wrenches, called a Badnor Wrench, by the way, and she was going to auction it in a special moment of her garage sale. She was one of these people these days who put on Garage Sales of Rolling Thunder, in which "lightning bursts of special offers" strike upon every hour to keep you inexorably browsing at the garage sale all the day long. Even when you found yourself stuck there inexorably looking at the stitching on Grandma's throw rug, you'd stay on. Even when you found yourself stuck there still inexorably several hours later with a surprise third beer the husband of the house gave you apologetically and there you are browsing over a child's boardgame like Connect Three thinking *I could still play this for fun*. People get these ideas about Rolling Thunder Garage Sales and such like from capitalism, which makes them try too hard.

And sure, you might find it impossible to believe that I'd cycle four hours to get only a chance at a Badnor Wrench, but I like to ride my bicycle so could we move past that topic, please? What I want to explain to you is that as I was sojourning past muffler shops and matriculated gas stations and the car washes like places where you pour water over your car for a momentary sparkle, I began to get a growing feeling of sunlit despair. Now, no one wants to hear about despair, least of all me, but bear with me as I explain this. Here in this sun-drenched kingdom where there's all this light, light, light filtering in to burn your brain out, where you wind up your whole day in the Laundromat washing away the dog-ness of your dog, here where you might look behind a bookshelf and be surprised by a full bottle of wine some mysterious someone left for you earlier in the year, here in this sun-spackled empire where they've left no room for a mere bicycle, there is now no reason for your despair to grow greater. And yet it does. Why so?

Here's why: I get down there to see the girl about the

wrench, or to even see the garage sale, and there's no garage sale whatsoever, they've packed up and left, there's only a couple old newspapers scattered in the driveway, a single cardboard box containing a single beat-up volume of the *Encyclopedia Britannica* (the volume with F in it, looked like), and some twists of that horrible twine that scratches your fingers idling with the newspaper. "Where are you?" I said aloud, regarding the girl. I at least wanted a chance to bid on the wrench. Oh, and plus it was supposed to be a Christian garage sale! I found my own newspaper, the nickel paper from between the washers, and fumbled vaguely with my cell phone until I got the number on the ad plugged in, and I texted in all caps: IT'S UNPROFES-SIONAL TO WRAP UP A GARAGE SALE EARLY ESPECIALLY WHEN YOU ADVERTISE A BADNOR WRENCH AUCTION JUST SO YOU CAN GO TO THE LAKE OR WHATEVER IT IS YOU'VE BLOWN OFF TO DO. I THOUGHT YOU WERE CHRISTIAN. GUESS NOT.

And yeah, that's the whole story. The moral? Sometimes you got to know you're full in the knowledge of your right-eousness to tell someone What For in a text. And I was so righteous that day, that just as I lowered my cell phone from my nearsighted eyes, just as I heard the sound effect of the text flying out to the satellite, I noticed someone had went and built a whole entire liquor store catty corner to the garage sale. Stuff like that, kiddos, it's like God reaching down and patting your back with his huge hand and telling you Good Job. Or Good Job, Son, And Never Mind These Pretenders as the case was that day. As in: Good Job Soldiering Through and You Deserve a More-Victorious-Than-it-Would-Otherwise-Be-Sober Ride Home.

- The End -

All of it Like Tension

Missed out on a bath, and so didn't catch on to the weekend like a sleeping dinosaur, the edge of heaven missed by an inch, the threat of time, always a threat, always a loggerhead, always uninspiring, never friendly. But Hart Fich, his wife frigid, unless he could con her into a drive in the country. In the country her mind let slip idle bursts of smiling, and then if he found a place to park behind an abandoned barn, or down some unkempt footpath and under the blue water sky, then he could tangle her panties out from under her while she kissed his neck and face all over, and Hart could then resolve his man curse with Mrs. Fich loving him every moment.

So on weekends country sojourns became ever more necessary, since Hart hated sex's vapor trail of useless thought, hated when it tapped insistently on his shoulder, or brainwashed him idly.

For Mrs. Fich, Mrs. Tandra Fich, it had become an issue in the dog walking to go out without her husband if he insisted on a blue windbreaker, or rather THE blue windbreaker. Hart's belief in napkins lay both fallow and shallow, and so food drifted from his mouth to the collar of his shirts and for some reason through several dining-out adventures the blue windbreaker had been landscape-blasted with food stains. Never to be washed lest it shrunk, the blue windbreaker became a song to a series of disap-pointments in napkin use. Her husband thought only of the trees he saved but she thought only of the society she kept while dog walking and so he was no longer allowed.

This was all of course a slow boat to epiphany for the Fiches becoming doggers, which are the people who pull into dog parks for sex in their cars. Not sex with the dogs, of course, but with the dogs looking on. Mrs. Fich got into that, which coupled with her love of country sex. Hart Fich had to occupy himself with other matters, then, when they were in the city, like matters like how Hart wanted to write a vampire novel wherein the vampires couldn't be killed with stakes to the heart, and they instead had to be killed by being struck by either cars or helicopters.

- The End -

All The Light

All the light and hearts afire cleaned his mind passages away, golden silt through a hundred sieves, and he therefore couldn't fish anymore. His neighbor fishermen (bar stools), each as short as the other, both their upper arm sets rounded the same. Both their hairpieces plastered makeshift doom down. He just tapped the fishing tackle box that didn't have a tangle of line coming out of it. The type of girl who lays her head on a bar provides the type of light he needs to not find joy in fishing any longer.

Why does he drink soda pop? To have flavor enter his mouth? Maybe it's the soda pop what's slushing his belly and keeping him from fishing. There was a freshwater pond there, and you'd get there just in time for the Portugese fishing fleet to get in and you'd buy your dinner right from the boat. His hands were cold from no circulation. He needed to be casting. He's got this calcium deficiency. On the other side is a neighbor (bar stool) who's a doppelganger. Simply one day met his twin in a bar. They were surprised at first but then they fell into easy discussion of getting a couple poles, a box of tackle, and just getting on down there to the docks, in spite of the presence of all this light. It's just that no one gets any sleep around here, pointed out his twin. But lack of sleep was not to stop them fishing. And all the others crowding the docks, he asked, all of them with hearts afire? Never mind them, said the twin, there's plenty of fish in the sea. He and his twin out on the docks with the sun too bright and the waves reflecting melancholy but they fished all the same, and the game of it took them through a good day. But then upon walking home the twin said the deaths of the fish were starting to bother him. He wasn't sure if he was beginning to see their little fishy souls in the depths of their dark eyes. He wasn't sure if all the sad push of all the light was just being unsure about killing anything at all anymore, even fish which had always hitherto seemed an okay thing to kill. And all the time the twin was talking he began to wonder if the twin was real, or just a fresh hallucination of his forever budding guilt.

- The End -

Alright

It's alright, whoever you are. Maybe all you can think about today, maybe all that's on your mind for the whole day, like maybe you don't get anything done and maybe all and everything that you can contemplate and chew over is just the way your sister stuck her pink shovel in the sand back when you two were kids. And that's alright.

- The End -

Ambulance Driver

Ambulance driver always contemplated running people over with his ambulance, and then driving back around the block and picking the people up.

But then through many quiet nights sat in the driver's seat of the ambulance in the ambulance garage, sifting through miniature bottles of rainbow liquors, the ambulance driver slowly came around to realizing he didn't work on commission.

He sat and sipped and thought: Now, that would be a good idea, if it were that the more people I bring into the hospital, the more money I get paid. But I get paid anyway. I get paid whatever happens. This is America! This is the year 2007! I get paid pretty damn good from the pockets of the sick! And sometimes nothing happens and I still get paid. I'll just sit here all night with Larry asleep beside me, and sometimes Larry falls into his deepest snoring sleep and I pull out a porn mag and have me a pud pull, and that's all that happens all the night through, and yet I still get paid. In fact, I guess it's lucky for the innocents of the world that I don't work on commission because then I'd run people down just in order to take them to the hospital and get paid the big bucks and Larry wouldn't say a thing or I'd wreck his house and fuck his wife.

- The End -

An Apartment With No Mirrors

Elton lived in an apartment with no mirrors. He still saw a lot of his hands and he still saw the rest of his body but he never quite knew the condition of his face. When he shaved he saw blood in the sink but fortunately he only bled rose petals. He saw the food he picked from his teeth. He didn't quite know how to smile.

Upstairs was the roof and downstairs was the neighbor. By rights, the roof belonged to Elton but he let the neighbor use it because she sunbathed without a top. She would ask Elton to come out and talk to her and he would come out, sweating and blinking. She'd ask him why he smiled funny and then she'd show him her teeth and say that that was how to smile.

Elton lay in bed at night and kneaded his sheets with his feet and hands and worried what his neighbor thought of him. Then his worry would turn to the spike-winged bats that clung upside down to the eave just outside his window. There were five of them, two grown-up bats and three little baby bats, and Elton worried mostly about how he had no way of telling if these bats were vampires.

- The End -

An Epidemic of Lemonade Stands

Capitalism is okay and everything, and it's okay to pass capitalism on to the next generation and everything, thought Moss, looking up and down his suburban street. *But today there is a lemonade stand at the bottom of every every every every every driveway.*

Moss sipped at his beer. *Hot beer is foul, but damn me to hell should I give in to that lemonade.*

- The End -

Ancestry

Fetterman had been trying to give the same plastic bag away to the last ten customers. Everyone came up with only one or two items they could easily carry without the bag, and so didn't want the bag. "They're bent on preserving the natural world," muttered Fetterman. The bag developed a million lunar wrinkles as it waited to be used and was crumpled by Fetterman's frustrated, equally lunar-wrinkled right hand. Pretty soon the bag would become undesirable as a bag, but Fetterman couldn't just throw it out, that would be wasteful. He might even have to take it home his own self. "One of these fuckers in the line better want the goddamn plastic bag," he muttered. Suddenly an old woman, quite possibly even older than Fetterman, arrived with nothing but a pile of cans of beans and Fetterman smiled a wizened smile. He deserved a break, after all, because it gnawed always at Fetterman that one of his great-great-great grandfathers had been justly killed by Indians. *Native Americans,* Fetterman corrected himself inside his head. *But he deserved it for sure,* Fetterman reminded himself inside his head. *He in fact asked for it.* Fetterman thought inside his head: *Maybe genealogy is too involving a hobby for me.*

"Could I have a paper bag, thank you?" said the old woman.

- The End -

Anglo Saxon Jurisprudence

Once a boy decided to sneak out to Bag Boy and I'm learning to tell a herring from the carp. Too late for dolls, who's died no one's died. An almond cookie? How'd you get them all the same size? Five minutes to international airspace. And so the occupants of the fake town in deepest Bulgaria came to live in America and pretended that all you have to do is call someone a funny face if he worked hard and didn't like you. 'Jeepers' they'd say back when bubblegum was popping their jaws, they'd say 'Jeepers' and that they like you okay, Johnny, and then that phrase evolved and advanced into a horror movie all the way toward the end of the '90s. Do you think it was a cyclone? He also scares me and he panics me. Why does she scream and cry and yell preposterous that she should be angry with him just because he was out with a client. Apparently in India they have a whole spiritual way of life, and it's now residing in the body of a child called Griselda Magump, a case unique in the annals of Anglo Saxon Jurisprudence. We in India are not afraid of death said the spiritual man with utmost arrogance. We have been parents and children and friends to one another, he added. You can still play with dolls if you're a boy. It's not too late if you're a thirty-, forty-year-old boy. Fifty. Ah remember now how you and your cousin occupied the trailer and crept into the lighted night of Alaska in order to sneak all that way to Bag Boy in its 24/7 status and you bought pretzels and you bought candy and you both gobbled these things in imitation of a party. That left your cousin fat right up to adulthood. That left you fat, too, but you'll never admit as much. Harnessing the compulsions of a child, be it boy buying girl toys, fat-boy-to-fat-be stuffing candy. But now, ah, we've not gotten past our feminine side when we ask the wife how she bakes an almond cookie all the same size as all the other almond cookies, but we have at least gotten past the candy in the local 24/7 store, because almond cookies after all.

- The End -

Animalia Ode to New Texas

Night is fallen in the castle, and a fox is doing his best southern accent, and the mice are free and the bunnies are free and the raccoons are even free and the cats aren't free but they don't much care. The throne room's on fire, and the lady in the orange-frame mirror has got a fancy lipstick job going steady. What's she doing here, being human and all? Nothing, she's just a picture, a mirage that they don't understand from humans being gone so long. The lion is muttering about miserable unfairness, sucking his thumb, and suddenly he has a go at his buddy the green snake, who is in turn busy watching a singing rooster amble by.

"Why don't you get yourself some legs," asks the lion bitterly.

"Oh, I'll just do that then," says the snake with deadpan sarcasm. How he hated the lion when the lion had quite obviously snuck out to get drunk on zebra blood. It was why they could never keep any zebras around.

A kitten arrived then, approached the throne. "Lion, I don't know what to do with myself," says the kitten. "I'm a shadow of you, a carbon copy." The lion rolls his eyes with the weight of leadership and the snake feels the burden and takes it. "Chase a mouse, but don't kill it nor catch it," the snake advises.

The kitten adjusts its face to a look of cuteness and satisfaction and the lion and snake can't help but smile sadly at similarities gone so deep as to be gone. Just like those pesky humans. Much the same at any rate.

- The End -

Announcer

Announcer sits at the bendy bar nursing his colorful cocktail, grimacing down into the casino. *Yeah, don't tax the super-rich,* he reckons. *Just watch them blow $5000 per hand of three-card poker, blow it away down the casino hole.*

Grim news from the world of sports, thinks the Announcer, gathering his thoughts for tomorrow's announcement. It's what he'll have to say that's bothering him, not how he'll say it, so of course he can try a few things in spite of how somewhere the staff writers whittle away. No, okay, it's bothering him because gosh how he used to love the ol' crack of the bat. *Grim news from the world of sports, sports fans, the sport of baseball has been closed down. You heard it here first, my dear sports fans. It's why I have a hangover this morning and I'm thinking about how baseball why baseball why baseball. But never mind my troubles as it's all over, indeed yes indeed, it's all over for baseball in an official capacity, not just in the ennui sense. It's been a dangerous game, for one thing. You could get hit in the head with the ball for example. Also, baseball players, when in high school, have a tendency toward bullying kids who aren't as strong as them. But the main problem is that there has been a lot of steroid use amongst the ball players. So they're not even actual baseball players actually playing baseball any longer. You do understand this don't you? Because we don't want you showing up in the stands any longer, sports fans. Those manic-tempered, heathen-eyed, snot-blowing rage machines of ravaged muscle and veiny necks are playing a drug-fueled hydra crazy superstrength noisemaker game of lights and supersurroundsound. WHACK BAT BALL etcetera and so on and now it's stopping. It's being stopped. It's no longer a working model or something to pass time nationally by. And it's not baseball. It's not baseball. Not baseball.*

Announcer nodded to himself. He stared into the maroon fractions of his drink. *Yeah, that's the way I'll lay it out,* he thought, heavy duty cloaking his slightly shaking shoulders.

- The End -

Anspach

Anspach was crawling down the line for the bus with his pitted eyes. Each time his gaze came to a Latino housekeeper, no matter her size or shape, Anspach tinkered with the shades of a scenario involving the housekeeper; raising the shades, lowering them. In the scenario he was a baron in one of the houses set against the hills above El Paso, and he would come into a certain room of his baronial mansion and catch the housekeeper swiping a wad of hundred-dollar bills that Anspach, as the baron, had hidden, and the swipe would come from a cookie jar, from a hook rain on a bookshelf-type thing, the swiping of the wad of hundred-dollar bills would be the swiping of the hundred-dollar bills from between the pages of a book Baron Anspach had hidden the wad of hundred-dollar bills in, for example. So Baron Anspach, upon capturing the housekeeper, would say: "You would steal from me? Then you will marry me and we will make your theft legal by making it wife-like."

A man broadsides Anspach's view of the line for the bus, a man at least five-feet wide. "There must've been some weather last night. I've never in my life seen snow on those mountains." Anspach looked where the man was pointing. Snow cloaks were indeed against and amongst a string of mountains Anspach didn't know the name of, just one of these collections of mountains up there in mountain-range spaces Anspach hadn't learned the name of unlike the kid in grade school who always knew the name of every state and every mountain and every state capital and every state of being and every state of shock. Which put Anspach in mind of a 45 record he had once.

Anspach grunted in response to the man, then skidded

his eyes so he didn't have to have a conversation. The man moved on. *Ah*, thought Anspach. *Poor fat fella just wanted a friend, and I snuffed him.* Anspach imagined the fella would kill himself or others in the end, out of loneliness. The poor fella speaking now to some other stranger on some other topic. Anspach continued thinking how he would sweep a housekeeper off her feet and how such sweeping would involve the philosophy that a housekeeper could be forgiven anything, anything at all.

- The End -

Answer

Did you get that part about the guy answering the phone? I know that guy in real life, and he would never accept a telephone call like that. That guy, I know him like I know my own name, that guy would never talk to anyone with that tone of voice, that guy would never talk to anyone who had those sorta half-racist remarks to make, that guy would never so much as lift up an old-fashioned receiver and stick it deafly to his ear if he knew someone like that was on the other end of the line, though of course really that's just metaphor, these lines have no beginning, no end, and of course they don't exist no more hardly at all.

- The End -

Answering Machine of Palanuk

The answering machine of Palanuk still existed as a viable answering machine. Here we are in the year 2050 and Palanuk still has an answering machine that works, tape and everything. Go on, stop sitting there at your desk wrecking paperclips because your co-workers hate you but are trying to be nice to you, go on, go on, call his home number, see what happens. You will almost certainly hear the following hymnal on his ancient answering machine:

> Since Christmastime of our last year
> I've missed my sweet good Jesus dear
> Every day I rise from tangled sheets
> And look between the fence-post pleats
> At the richest people in America
> And if I'm not there with them, in America
> I go to work the day away
> In the fields where my Lord holds
> swaaaaaaaaaayyyyyyyyyyyyyyy

If, on the other hand, you get Palanuk on the phone, you will hear him praising the Lord for each bite of his breakfast, for each rustle of wind under a leaf outside the window, for each twist of phrase from you that he finds pleasing, and this bubbling over of praise even though money, right now, for Palanuk, is quote unquote 'kinda tore up', even though he'll at first be talking to you and sound rude with a 'who is this?' or a 'who are you?' you'll eventually get a 'God bless this' or a 'God bless that' or a 'God bless you' out of him, and a 'God bless you' from his Spanish lips sounds so very pleasant, so very romantic, be you man or woman.

But hang up on his answering machine. You're about to be fired. 10 minutes until you get fired. Make 10 sales and you won't be fired. Sit here a fool with your phone in your hand. You've got 10 minutes to turn this job around in your favor.

- The End -

Any Four Minutes

What can we do, little Biott, in our four-minute wait for the Caledonian Train? How about a history? Oops, three minutes now, best be quick. Blood has been shed on these tracks at some time or another, little Biott, if you think of everything in this bit of space happening all at once. Blood shed here at some point or another. Not a very original thought, I know, but that's what happens with haste. Make your own story in your own mind now. Two minutes. Time passes slowly while you're waiting for a train, Biott, but don't get anxious, your entire life will vanish quite quickly, even before you know it's gone. Two minutes still. Yeah, little Biott, when you're on your deathbed, think back to how bored you were waiting for this very train, so bored indeed that you took to tediously imagining blood on the tracks at my cue, and think there on your someday deathbed: "Gee, what I wouldn't give to be back there bored and imagining cultural phrases as happenings and waiting on that train in the hot eternal afternoon."

- The End -

Any Moment

Learning to drive in later life leads to the question of why anyone would want to drive. Why would anyone want to drive? Looksee, when you're a teenager it's exciting to keep track of turn signals and where other cars are and have been and are soon and are going to be later on, which is the same as where they are soon. You get so used to the danger when you're a teenager that you immediately start driving drunk.

But being a grown-up and for the first time learning to drive your safety nodules are entrenched, and you quickly become agitated and apprised of how complicated the whole operation of driving is, and how dangerous it is, and how that danger makes you nervous. If you learn to drive later in life you are guaranteed to find yourself someday on the highway thinking: "Oh my God! Oh my God! We're all driving in these cars at 60 miles per hour! Oh my Dear Sweet God!"

At any moment you might be in an accident when you're in a car. When you're a teenager you're immortal and it doesn't matter if you're in an accident and it's even an idealized idea to be in an accident, especially in songs from the 1950s. But learn to drive when you're old and staid and past the age of 20 and all you can think is: "Holy Mary Mother Of God! Oh my God! We're all driving at 60 miles per hour and there's no track we're on! There's nothing to keep us from veering into one another at any second and exploding! Oh Sweet Jesus Lord do you realize how fast 60 miles per hour is?!"

They should not have invented cars. It might have been better just to keep things slow with having invented golf carts. Henry Ford invented the golf cart before the car because he was an avid golfer, golfing all the time with his rowdy friends, and he should have stopped with inventing the golf cart and not moved on to inventing the car. Yes, sure, if you're a teenager you think cars are a great invention and you can be inducted into the idea of driving cars no problem, but that's because you're a stupid teenager. You grow up even slightly, and realize even slightly how little sense some things make, and THEN you learn how to drive, and that's a big problem.

I'm not talking about myself. Listen, I'm not talking about myself. I was one of the "normal" ones. I was taught to drive as a teenager. I learned to love road trips. I had to concentrate very hard to learn to drive home while drunk from Everclear early on in my driving career, when I was still but a teenager. I thus learned to drive flip, to drive fly. And by the way, it's never a good idea to drive drunk. I strongly do NOT recommend driving drunk. Any teenagers reading this manifesto should NOT get any stupid ideas and drive drunk. Anybody else reading this manifesto should NOT get any stupid ideas about driving drunk. Driving drunk isn't so bad if you get yourself killed, because if you're driving drunk you've automatically got a footnote of suicide somewhere inside. But driving drunk IS bad if you get some innocent someone killed who didn't want to die. And that's the real problem with drunk driving. Also the other problem with drunk driving is that Jesus H. Christ On A Sidecar operating a motor vehicle while sober is horrifying enough, why in the Christ Name of Heaven Above and God's Name Too That We Must Not Utter would you ever in a million years want to get into a spine-tinglingly horrifying motor vehicle and drive it around <u>DRUNK?!</u> on top of the fact you're even driving it around in the first place? That's the same exact thing as if you stood at a window you had to clean and cleaned the window while simultaneously screaming and screaming and screaming until you lost your voice and the cops came to your house. Same exact thing.

Point is: I'm not talking about me. I'm talking about a cousin of mine. He learned to drive at age 30, and all my cousin would ever say to you, while you rode along in his car's passenger seat, was thus: "Oh my God! Do you see all these crazy sons of guns?! They're all in metal cans! They're all going 60 miles per hour! They're all around us! We're going 60 miles per hour, too! Oh my Sweet Mary Mother of Jesus God Lord! How do people think they can live in this horrible world drunk?! I can barely live in this horrible world sober! Oh my God look at that car! Look at what he is doing! Oh Lord God on the Throne in Heaven with Baby Jesus on His Lap why do people drive in these car things?! Get me out of this car! Where's an exit?! Oh my God my speedometer just went up to 65! Sweet Hallucinating Jesus Horsefeathers Christ!"

That's what riding in the car with my cousin was like when he was driving. That's all he'd say, those sorts of things. Otherwise, if you were walking in a field with him talking about how he wanted to plant corn, not fake corn but real corn, he'd be fine.

- The End -

Anymore

When you have a dog or an infant you'll find yourself in these conversations involving a single name: "Hamish!" you will yell "Hamish!" I see it happen every day. I hear it happen, more like. Now it happens to me. "Clyde!" I yell. "Clyde!" I call. There's something delicious about it, and there's of course love in it. Communication or more often only attempted communication with an Other.

I'm just here guarding this pipe, making sure it doesn't leak more. My eyes are bright and my mind is excited. I'm always amazed at how the boss knows what the pipes might do if they're not watched close and has a dogsbody like myself at the ready for the guarding.

How is it Big Timothy got four chocolate biscuits to our one plain Tesco biscuit apiece? I and the boss even. Big Timothy comes in here for a few measly days of chippie tinkering and the lady of the house, buxom and hot-eyed even though she's well into her eighties, has given him four chocolate biscuits. Oh of course, how stupid of me, there it is. One of those moments where you're repeating the puzzle to yourself and you realize the answer.

In those days of building houses I acquired a dog. This dog has become the love of my life. I would sooner jump in front of a bus then lose the presence of this creature. I might have to Romeo & Juliet it with this dog someday. I have never known a more puzzling love, but I don't mean that I don't equally puzzlingly love other humans (certain ones of them that I'm related to or have gotten married to or just like and love), it's just that I've never known something so puzzling as the love of a dog because I can't BLAH BLAH BLAH BLAH BLAH BLAH BLAH all day with this dog about the sense of love. That's what's profound. Unspoken love, etc. Hey, if you love a dog, I don't have to explain any of this to you, and it's exactly the type of BLAH BLAH BLAH I'm scolding. In fact, this scree is for dog lovers only. Anyway, we acquired this dog, the blue-eyed wife and I.

We drove out beyond the farmlands and then back into where the people live in their driveways so to avoid property taxes, seriously, they build whacking great vaulting structures and drive around in off-road vehicles finding roads in the dark and giving each other contact highs with major growths of marijuana in glowing, tin-foiled closets they show off at parties only to probably wish they hadn't shown them off in the dull gray of the next morning. Out here a redheaded lady tells me and my doll of a wife (who's English) that she (the redheaded lady) has a Corgi for us to take with us, just like the Queen's (who's English). This redheaded lady is never to be trusted for her absolute enthusiasm and joie de vivre, but I suppose $50 for a session onstage is okay in the end, which is what the redheaded lady had paid me for my session onstage. The Big Time, etc.

To take us to her house in its secret, tax-free location, she piles us into the back of a boat that's hitched to the back of the trailer and I think into the future about how that terrorist is going to hide bleeding in a boat in the dead of Boston's winter, and gosh how cold it will be to hide there knowing in his heart of hearts that all he's managed to kill is a child instead of killing an entire corporation, and all he's doing right then is waiting for inevitability to manifest the inevitable for all those cold, cold hours. We can't stick our heads up because the redheaded woman is driving too fast into the wind, and we'll get bugs whipped in our faces for the boat's lack of windshield. "This is crazy, we don't know where we're going," says my wife in a whisper like sunshine, as we roll around together in the bottom of the boat, especially when the vehicle pulling it, which I didn't get a good look at, goes off road and is bumping over stones half-buried and tree roots and whatever else you get where you don't have a road in the wilderness because you're fleeing taxes.

Finally we arrive at the redheaded lady's so-called farm and fall out of the boat all stiff from the cold and bruised from being thrown around. "This dog better be a good one," says my wife and I smile because she makes me smile. I'm only entertaining the notion of a dog because it's Christmas and my wife likes dogs, but I'm not serious. But then all of a sudden I am serious, and it's not the Corgi but another dog, a black bounding thing that runs low and smiles big, and is half of a Dachshund and half of a Poodle. He speaks in our minds and says how he's been waiting for us all this time. It happens fast from there. He's in my wife's arms and licking her cheek and she's laughing. I will never forget the image in that last sentence I just wrote as long as I live; it is the happiest image I have in my mind's eye. We book this black curly bundle of rolling joyful dog for a week and if we want to bring him back we can but I look into the future and know we'll be in love with him within a day. Then we're back in the back of the boat and being pulled along the same route in reverse, but we know where all the bumps are going to be from the mirror of our minds and this time we're stabilized at all the right moments. We hug to each other, my wife and I, and between us is this dog smiling and skittering between us and licking at us like a wild pickle in a sandwich or some other metaphor, and everyone and everything in the bottom of that boat is all I ever need anymore.

- The End -

Appreciate Ya

"I appreciate ya," Halo Phillips would say, even while he was madder than an old wet hen, even while he had his modem propped up on a couple of boxes in a shelf in a window in the northeast corner of his apartment, there behind a leather chair with the closet opened and never closed and all that to get it to connect to the INTRAWWW. He'd asked the INTRAWWW company to come around to his house, and the technician had been there, handling the modem like a divining rod, wandering the house looking for a signal like looking for Jesus or looking for water or like Jesus probably looked for water the night before a miracle. Now the modem was set atop the boxes, shelf, in the corner, behind the chair, closet door open and never closed, and it was certainly a jury-rigged path to INTRAWWW service, certainly. But Halo still went through his harshest conversations on the numbing inconveniences of lame modernity to finish them with "I appreciate ya." He'd say as much should you speak to him from the service department of this fake company from which we were all speaking back then.

Halo especially appreciated Magdalena, a wrong number he'd gotten on his cellular phone, and now she called him all the way from Texas to call him baby doll, but even that and even Halo's unstoppable cheerfulness supported by "I appreciate ya" was not enough to keep away the dirge of the day. Funerals had nothing on that first pure cold day of winter. As in: summer's over. Halo would say as much, he'd say to your enthusiasm: "I appreciate your enthusiasm for this Intra Double-ya Double-ya Double-ya, but I can't share your enthusiasm, now how can I when all I got is this first dark day of winter making me feel like I'm meant to be at someone's funeral and someday soon that someone will be me. God, kid, don't let anyone bury you in Idaho, you'll freeze in the ground every winter, it's cold enough down there when there's no sun, even if they buried you in Florida."

Boy, you listen to Halo and you start thinking about whether you want to be cremated and you're thinking about that, what, 40 years too soon? (Hopefully.)

So I want to say here a reply I could never make to him at the time: "Ah, but Halo, and your dying faith, you must remember how winter bodes coffee and every other entertaining hot drink ever thought up by them uniting steam and water and flavor. You could even say you must appreciate coffee. At least, Halo, appreciate coffee."

- The End -

Arbor Madness

Palm trees are known as The Idiocy of L.A., the arbor madness some loser brought over here from some Indonesia place (where the palm trees were meant to be), and they don't even belong, neither the palm trees nor the losers. Hollywood is for winners. No one knows who that mysterious non-arboreal-leaning freak was but he should not have done what he did because palm trees are infamous for killing other trees. And it was probably a real-estate agent who did it; they'll do anything to sell a house regardless of botany. Selling real estate back in those days when the palm tree was brought in—like a contagious man with Ebola wrapped in bandages in a wheel chair with one flat tire—wasn't particularly difficult, plenty of free land lying around, but just not enough buyers, and with homes back then they didn't have room indoors needs-wise for anything else besides people, they certainly didn't have room indoors for anything like intelligence or a reasonable sense of humor. It's one of those things where you try and get someone else to do it until you can get up the gumption to do it yourself. You ever see a palm tree reach next door to itself and strangle a pine? I have. I thought it was a monster movie or a dream but it was real. You ever see a woman in a slumhouse chuck a lit rag out the window to kill the palm tree lurking there, and the whole palm tree burns down like a tower in some old drinking-game movie? I have. I've stood on that very bridge over by Alvarado watching a palm tree go down in flames. I've had music in my ears that I couldn't stop dancing to even when I had to go out on a bicycle under those very palms. They loom like nerves and you look at them up close under a microscope and they can snatch you. Or when their armlessness gets in the way of snatching they just summon up their buddies the Joshua Trees. Those.

This is all by way of explaining what happened to my grandfather when he was 80 years old or more. He was in the twilight of himself, at that age, and so he didn't have time to do things that needed to be done anymore, those sundry items like for example he noticed the palm tree in his backyard had extended one root far enough through the ground to put a crack in the side of the swimming pool. But he didn't have the energy to do anything about it, did he? So the root of the palm tree of course began leaking palm tree oil into my grandfather's swimming pool and as we all know but my grandfather didn't, when you mix palm oil and chlorine it is the most toxic substance known to man. If you were to stand in a bath of sulfuric acid mixed with raw uranium mixed with Drano (which is a type of drain cleaner currently on the free market in America), you couldn't do any worse for your physiology than swimming in a swimming pool full of chlorine mixed with palm oil. Which is exactly what my grandfather did, all because he couldn't be bothered to chop down a palm tree, and that's why my grandfather is dead today.

Which brings us to the summation of this scree: palm trees are the most evil tree known to man, you should look on them with distrust, hatred, and when you're done doing that you should shy away from them if not avoid them at all costs and also campaign to have them all destroyed. Or as a botanist once told me: "Listen, kid, if any tree needs to go extinct, it's the motherfucking palm tree." Thank you for your time.

- The End -

Are Dead

Had a Hollywood dream of riding in the white pickup with my Dad while I spoke on a cell phone to Phillip K. Dick and Remy Gault regarding whether they had stories to sell to Hollywood. Phillip K. Dick had nothing memorable to say (in that infuriating way of dreams being just stupid, stupid dreams) and Remy Gault said he was living in Bar Harbor, and when my Dad overheard that part of the conversation he smiled. My Dad was always into harbors. Trouble with such a dream is that my Dad's dead, Phillip K. Dick and Remy Gault are dead, and the pickup's been sold. Trouble with such a dream is that I'm not even sure who Remy Gault is, I think he was the mayor of a French town in the 1800s in a book either fiction or non-fiction I once read, but anyway whoever he is, he's probably dead. Trouble with such a dream is they keep telling me to keep a Dream Diary but Jesus H. Christ, why? Seriously: why?

- The End -

Are You a Devil?

They were in a Chinese restaurant, one of those. The floor was decorated with black, torn-apart stars, one of those floors. Really you couldn't tell what was lint and what were the torn-apart stars. So she felt the floors needed mopping. But the table was good. Each cup, dish, and silverware surface on the table glinted kindly. Her eyes, toward him, did not. "Are you a devil, and did you fool me?" she asked, without any religion.

✍

In bed, thirty-three nights prior, his spackled arms wrapping her, he'd whispered in Thora's ear: "What if we robbed the bank? You and I. Together. A Kentucky-Made team. You stay and duck the heat so you don't screw up Sally. But then when the heat's off you come join me in Guadalcanal."

✍

Three years prior, she'd already at last admitted to herself that this was going to be her boyfriends' way with her. Thora Bailey (her) was a bank teller. That wasn't enough income to support sweet little Sally, so Thora was also a stripper on Saturday nights. She didn't prefer the bank to the strip club, or the strip club to the bank; there were the same amount of money germs in each place, and as far as she was concerned money had, too, a withering smell, and she wasn't quite sure exactly why the world needed it in these modern times. She wasn't an economist or nothing, so maybe she just didn't have the whole appreciation aspect, but she figured money was an outmoded concept, the same as war. Nothing that smelled so bad and felt so rife with germs, every last piece of it, nothing like that could be benevolent.

✍

Between the strip club and the bank, it was the boyfriends Thora Bailey met at the club who always wanted to rob the bank and the boyfriends she met at the bank who she'd catch sneaking into the club.

Of the half of the boyfriends who suggested robbing the bank, only half were in earnest. But a quarter of her boyfriends seriously wanting to rob the bank was plenty.

✍

She'd wound up being the insider on four bank robberies. 1992, 1997, 1999, and this latest one in 2002. This latest one sometimes seemed the most pointless, because the boy wasn't even cute and had hair that wouldn't stay put no matter how much she licked her fingers and slapped at it, and she wasn't even sure if she liked him or loved him.

✍

"What if we robbed the bank? Like, seriously. I'm serious. I'm not a bank robber. I only robbed, like, eight gas stations when I was a teenager. But I'd bank rob this one time since you're the bank teller and you'd have an in, right? Look, don't tell on me for asking about the bank, because I love you. But isn't there, like, a way you can think of to do it?"

✍

With each robbery the FBI had interviewed Thora, and before the interviews she'd find some quiet corner and sing this song to herself:

The bank
is a mighty old tank
I pulled
a wonderful prank
The bank
is a silly little tank
They've only got
themselves to thank

The song was only those eight lines long, and its style and content and tune and scansion needed some work. But it calmed her, and she'd go through those FBI interviews like they were stoned conversations at the beauty parlor.

✍

Thirteen years before the three years before the thirty-three nights before the night in the restaurant, skipping school all the while, Thora had kissed her first love, Spike Mongini, under the overpass on a foggy day just before the snow came. The air had a bracing but melancholy scent. That scent. In this air, her fresh hickeys had stung. After they'd kissed a long while, the two of them had smoked a third of a pack of clove cigarettes, except for two cigarettes they'd given to Teddy Morton when Teddy had come by mooching, Teddy the squirming, gimpy kid that no one liked, a kid with one blue eye open and one blue eye that opened halfway and gloves that never stayed put and a coat that hung torn between being a coat and being useless. Teddy stood and smoked with them and asked questions that Thora thought were at once annoying and cute. Spike just thought they were annoying, and when Teddy finished his second cigarette, Spike punched him in the stomach, and Teddy puked.

✍

Three years before that Thora was watching a lemonade stand for her best friend Sally. Sally had left Thora in charge of the cashbox and run into her house to, as Sally put it: "Make a different lemonade!" Teddy Morton had come along and wheedled Thora into just letting him have a cup of lemonade for free. He'd shambled off and when Sally emerged Thora had told her about the freebie. Sally had finally gotten too angry and their friendship had withered from there, like capitalism did to friendships back in those early days of understanding. Thora felt guilty about it until years later, when she'd named her daughter Sally in unspoken apology.

✍

Sally's father had been one of the bank robbers. Like the other bank robbers, he had fled with the money to Central America and never spoken to Thora again. Thora at last got a sense of humor about it with this latest boyfriend. She took him out to dinner the night before the robbery and delivered the line she'd thought about and practiced since three days before.

They were in the Chinese restaurant and Thora said: "Are you a devil, and did you fool me?"

"What?" said the boyfriend, with a mouthful of steamed rice.

Thora smiled sadly at him. "I just want to know, before

after tomorrow, when I never see you again."

The boyfriend swallowed. "What are you talking about? What do you want to know?"

"If you're a devil, and if you've fooled me."

The boyfriend rolled his eyes and stared into space, mimicking thinking.

Then he said: "No. I love you, and I love your girl Sally. I want to be her dad. I want to marry you in a Mexican church. Mexican weddings are more fun that American weddings. Plus American weddings don't count because Americans are all mean-ass about just who can get married and who can't. Anyway, you'll see. We'll meet up in Baja and you'll see."

✍

Three months later, Thora was getting off a bus and into the boyfriend's waiting arms. Even with a tan, he still wasn't cute, but oh well. Sally was riding piggyback, holding tight to Thora's shoulders. Summer had just begun, and Guadalcanal was as deliciously hot as she'd always hoped. The boyfriend had thought of the future and found Sally a pediatrician and a school, and he had found them all a bare white house in the sad bald sun, down near the beach where the sea lions appeared once a year.

✍

Thora wondered if merely the mulled-over and overly-conjured line she'd said had jinxed his abandoning her. She liked to think not. She liked to think they'd had a stronger bond. And the way they'd met by accident, out of the blue, in the cigar shop that one day. A cigar shop of all places. She'd been buying a cigar for her strip club boss's birthday.

Her future man had been buying a cigar for his dead dad. That had been good fortune enough, hadn't it? Anyway, the real surprise of it all as far as Thora was concerned was the boyfriend being who he was, Teddy Morton, the one and the same, and successful at nothing of life except for a taste for cigars that led him to her and an ability to rob one bank without capture.

✍

"Teddy," Thora whispered into his neck, then bit him a little. The sounds of Guadalcanal were around them. Sally was tugging at Thora's print dress.

- The End -

Aren't Guns Fun?

Aren't Guns Fun? was a simplistic movie compilation I saw late last night. It was of bare bald facts. I guess you'd call it a documentary, technically. Isn't that what they call it these days? I really don't know much about movies. It was just this movie with lists and lists of facts about guns. I sat in the movie theater with my popcorn slushing out my belly, but the images on the screen put me off the popcorn with fair rapidity. Usually I like popcorn but not enough to go to the stupid movies for it. This documentary also had re-enactment depictions of shooting sprees, wherein they'd re-enact one shooting spree after another, and explain 'why' the person who did it did it, why the person wasn't treated for mental illness, where they got the gun, etc. Also there were little biographies about the people getting killed in the shooting massacre spree things. The little biographies about the people made me wet-eyed. All without music. I kind of spent some time crying for some of those people, especially all the cute little kids that got shot to death. It was a very bald movie, very plain-spoken, just all these facts about guns and the people killed with guns, all of it repeated tonelessly. There was no one else in the theater or so it seemed at first but as I got adjusted to the dark and got exhausted/traumatized by all the facts about guns, I began to look around and counted at least ten other people watching this movie, all of them wearing black ties, which was weird. Even the women in the audience wore black ties, albeit fashionably. Anyway, I tried not to look around too much because you know how it is when you stare at someone watching a movie and they catch you watching and stare back. Awkward.

To keep my sanity in the movie theater, I had to relegate

myself to thinking about how guns had affected my own life, but I couldn't really think of a single instance. Well, I could think of one single instance. I had shot a squirrel with a .22 rifle as a kid and watched it die horribly and that was that, no more guns for me. And I've never needed a gun. The one time I had a mugger try to mug me I used my fists and hurt him so much I saw it in his eyes (the hurt) and he ran away. I felt bad about that, because he was obviously mugging me for some sad-and-horrible-failure-of-the-social-contract reason. I should've just given him the 600 bucks in my wallet. What's 600 bucks? So I felt bad about that but I'm glad I didn't, at least, kill the mugger with a gun. Yeargh! Gives me the shivers to think about it. Yeah, I'm glad I never killed another human being with a gun. My Dad was in the Vietnam War and I've every reason to believe he killed several human beings with guns and he didn't like that one bit, and he never talked about it, and he never let me join the army when I tried. Boy, I never saw my Dad so angry as when I talked about joining the army that one time. He didn't like that, not one bit. You should've seen how red his face got. Angry. And he didn't like that he'd been in the Vietnam War at all. No sir. He had no nostalgia for that. Also, I've never needed to hunt for my food because they have food in the supermarket. Cheap food, even, for when I've been poor, and so I've never been poor enough to need to hunt for my food and anyway they have supermarkets. Cheap food even if you're super poor, like Top Ramen. I love noodles. Did I tell you I love noodles? So I couldn't really speak to their value, guns I mean, I couldn't really speak to the value of guns except to say I've never needed one and I surely couldn't bear to watch that squirrel die back then. I still see that squirrel dying in moments of great depression and suicidal feeling even though that was almost 30 years ago. I guess I'm one of those sensitive types that you see going around writing stories and stuff and being sensitive.

The Maids was the double feature last night, a movie about hotel maids puzzling out the things they find in hotel rooms to illuminate the convergence of man and God. I picked up my popcorn again for that movie. It was fun to watch maids puzzling the mysteries of the universe out with slivers of soap and single socks and patterns of hairs on bathroom surfaces and discarded magazines. Who doesn't want to see such a movie?

- The End -

Argentina

Fly 5000 miles to Argentina.
Squeeze 100 pounds.
Badger crazy beats grizzly bear.

Used to be you could smoke cigarettes here at the High Desert Museum. You could smoke in the cafes, all along the phony woodland path, all whilst leaning over the otter exhibit. Then some p p p p (dare I say it?) then some penis went and burned half the museum down. It was made of wood and dry as conspiracy seating and hot as chapped thighs, sure, but all that penis had to do was be careful of his cigarettes instead of ruining it for everyone else. Luckily when the museum got burnt down halfway most of the animals there at the time worked together to escape in a rather spectacular show of Talent for Escapes. The baby porcupine used its quills to make the baby fox spring the rope wall. The snakes broke the glass with their fangs. The fish switched themselves from cold-blooded to warm-blooded and didn't mind their boiling aquariums.

But gone are those days. Sorry, I have this tendency to wishful thinking. I have this tendency to go without food in order to smoke my cigarettes. I learned the trick from an insurance salesman who was writing a pornographic film in Utah because he wanted to elevate pornographic films to The Level Of Art. I didn't know about that idea but I did know that No Food in Exchange for Cigarettes was a fandamntastic plan of attack. Just like how I managed to pause and watch the sun set on my 29th year in this world, just like how I managed to pause and watch the sun set on my 20s. Can't remember the way the sun was setting that day, in particular, because I was high as a kite, but I did what I could, didn't I? I made the memory for my memory banks, for what that was worth. Boy, my 20s. They started off with a snort of cocaine and ended much the same. Good thing for that sunset being half of a bookend. Because of course I should've watched the sunrise on the morning of my 20th birthday, which I definitely didn't, I was too busy dropping a tab of acid on my way into the gates of Disneyland. Bad idea, by the way, don't ever ever ever ever ever ever do that, drop acid and go to Disneyland (on your birthday no less). Seriously. They got cameras.

You know what though, about Disneyland? You used to be able to smoke in Disneyland, and even on the rides. I certainly am not kidding. You used to be able to have a leisurely cigarette on Space Mountain, I kid you not. Because once you get used to Space Mountain by riding it a few times in a row it's easy to smoke a cigarette on. Or it would've been, back in the day when you could smoke a cigarette on it. It's just that first hill of the rollercoaster thingie and then you can smoke, and you can even smoke going up that first hill if you're okay to smoke with all those lights. It is a truly bad idea that I'm not suggesting, by the way, to nowadays dare to smoke a cigarette on Space Mountain. Because they got cameras, and you will seriously never see the light of day again as long as you live once you're arrested for that cigarette. Also, probably, they probably banned smoking on rides at Disneyland because of that one time the Haunted House ride burned down with everyone in it. 116 people died in that fire. Bet you didn't hear about that. That's because of the Disneyland Code Of Silence. They hush it up real quick when there's been so much as a single death in the park, let alone a mass burning of 116 hapless tourists like happened that day.

Anyway, all this talk of Disneyland makes me miss Mom and Dad.

Seriously, the High Desert Museum, Disneyland, Utah, these are places that remind me of childhood and how I had so much potential. I was bursting with potential when I was 5 years old for example; the world was my oyster. And then I went and started smoking, I dropped acid willy nilly, I called out people by the technical terms for their genitals.

What else did I do? Oh yes, cocaine, I mentioned that.

I have had nothing to offer the world for years except a whole lot of warnings because I don't want to see anyone else hurt. And I especially don't want to think of innocent animals trapped in a fire, let alone tourists who don't know where they are in the first place, let alone mechanical ghosts. Somehow, I'm not sure which is sadder, of the three.

Are you?

- The End -

Arnie Spent Hours

Arnie spent hours in the Haight-Ashbury, looking for an inexpensive but elegant pot pipe to give his newlywed friend Barry.

"Sir? Excuse me?"

Arnie regarded the shadowy man with paranoia.

"Is this Haight Street?"

"Yeah. This is it," Arnie said. He wanted to add the interrogative word *Disappointed?* but he tactfully did not.

"Thanks," said the shadowy man.

Arnie finally bought a clay pipe that came in a velvet bag. An incisive twelve dollars plus tax for his jobless self. He drove it down to San Jose at breakneck speed. He was late with the present, really. Barry had been married for six weeks.

But Barry didn't seem too thrilled with the pipe. He just looked at it, as he and Arnie sat at Barry's brand new cherrywood kitchen table. Then Barry half-smiled and said: "Thanks."

It was the second time Arnie had heard the word in the past twenty-four hours. It was then Arnie realized that his and Barry's days of partying were over.

Arnie also realized that the shadowy people of The Haight often mistook The Haight for elsewhere than they were.

- The End -

Artist

It turned out the artist had to do one last charcoal pencil fucking drawing in a whiskey cloud this one last drawing being of her black-and-white cat she didn't want to do even one more charcoal pencil drawing because she'd just done a whole fucking speed-fueled fucking 400-piece series of them but she had to do it because the charcoal pencils were all she had that would work for drawing a decent picture of the cat for the cat's LOST poster and the artist missed the cat terribly but it took until nighttime to do the drawing when she'd meant to have it done by noon she made photocopies of the LOST CAT poster while tottering against the copier sneezing and burping tequila in the all-night newsagent then she kept the original drawing mailed one copy to herself in a date-stamped envelope stuck the rest of the copies up all over the neighborhood a few days went by someone came across one of the posters and studied it then a week later that same someone found the cat feasting behind a pub on a disemboweled pigeon the someone went back to get the phone number off the poster but the artist had gone around tearing the posters down in a fury of gin and misery over her cat which the artist was certain by that time was dead so this someone who found the cat had a decent, if skittish, new cat and the artist had nothing.

- The End -

At Night

At night the giant would stick its eye to the hole through his television and watch him as he slept.

He would go up against inanimate objects, versus walls etcetera, and always win emotionally even though the inanimate objects won physically.

He'd always smile if he saw someone he recognized.

It was never too long before he talked too much and said something stupid.

He took this nighttime job fliering for music shows. The job was hatched out of the back of a fly-by van that would stop in front of his house...

...him, his, we keep saying, let's call him !!Morrison!!

...back of a fly-by van that would stop in front of Morrison's house, Morrison's funny little house with its two gables painted to look like the eyes of the giant, with its purple walls and yellow shingles. You'd grin if you saw it, and maybe murmur 'cool'. The van would toot and Morrison would come out and knock on the back of the van and the door would swing wide and there'd be Pike, 'like the fish,' as Pike would tell you, and Pike would be chewing half-heartedly away at a cigarette. Pike sat in a wound-up, hunched, utterly awkward position, probably on the wheel well of the van for what Morrison could guess by his vantage point, and Pike was just about invisible in the universe of papers and notebooks and overstuffed cardboard boxes and building materials and wayward tools and television sets and outdated technologies that choked the van's back. Pike would rummage in a box and hand Morrison a teetering stack of fliers, and Morrison would manage to snug the fliers between one hand and his hairless chin. Morrison would feel the glossiness of the top flier at the tip of his chin, and he'd smell the freshness of the minting of the fliers. They were always fliers for raves in warehouses for where pillheads could go and eat pills and either dance all night or watch lights all night or nod to the beats all night, or maybe all three of those things. "Alright, Pike?" Morrison would ask. "Yessir," Pike would respond, rummaging. Then in the time it took for the fliers to be pulled from a box and handed over, Morrison would task himself to come up with one quick question about some other aspect of the van's contents, because of course the contents always fascinated. "What's with those bendy pipes?" Morrison would ask, for example. And Pike would respond one of three ways, he'd respond with obfuscation: "They're for another job." Which meant the universe of the van's contents was in turn responsible for a universe of this and that. Or Pike would respond with a correction: "They're not bendable." Or Pike would respond with the actual answer, always adding some tantalizing yet mysterious detail: "They're for gutters at The Channel Shed." And then the fliers would be handed over and Pike would give the same instruction, always the same instruction: "Only dole them out between midnight and five in the morning, right?" And then the van doors would swing shut and the van would drive away. Morrison would stand there wondering about the job's hours, wondering if the operation was just simply shy about fliering, wondering how Pike made the van doors swing shut without touching them. Or Morrison would wonder what such things as The Channel Shed could possibly be. Or Morrison would simply, with his free hand, snap his fingers in self-damnation at not asking what was always his biggest question after the van drove away. He'd then sing the short tuneless bit he'd made up his own self in regards to the question...

Who is he who drives that van?
Or is he a he, even a man?
Who is that driving that van?
And does he drive by a coda
Kicking at a can
He chucked that can of soda
On his driver's-side floor
Now it's in the way of the accelerator
Who is he who drives that van?
And why do I always first think of him as a man...?

Anyway, Morrison would deliver the fliers at night.

He thought of another van he and his friends had once captured in the countryside, and then they couldn't remember where they'd captured it.

He drove a vehicle he thought was like a van but much smaller, it could only fit him and the fliers and it did not run on gas, thank God.

He would always like to spot lonely soda cans sat lonely in empty parking spaces.

He would always like the radio to waver between stations with the stations belting out and then little interstices of static, the best time of this being the time the radio wavered between French people talking and Early American banjo blues.

Morrison pitched a tent in his yard so to avoid sleeping in front of the television and have the giant sticking an eye to the other side of the screen and go all night keeping the eye on poor Morrison. But then Morrison was always reluctant to go outside and sleep in the tent because it wasn't a good night's sleep.

But then again, neither was The Midnight Fliering Gig (as Morrison sometimes called it with capital letters in his thoughts and thoughts only), and creeping Morrison would go, down this street, down that, a prize when he found an apartment building with a stack of mailboxes, a pen in his pocket, a star in his eye, his heart chugging, his mother far away. The fliers went into mailslots. Every decent door had a mailslot. Mailslots could stand up straight and those were difficult to shove a flier through. Or a mailslot would be lying flat on the door but still have two opposing clusters of fibers beyond the squeaky mailslot threshold, and Morrison's hand would get tangled. But mostly, mostly, mailslots lay flat and were easy to feed. Morrison would slink along, feeding the fliers. He was good at it, and the fliers, reconfigured from a stack between his palm and chin to a load in a small cloth canvas bag, would whisper into mailslot oblivion oh-so-quickly, and Morrison might be done fliering by as early as three a.m.

He remembered how she had said: "Yes but always to soon become an endless series of lakes and waterfalls and mountains and none of it anywhere any home in sight."

He remembered how she would always be assisted by so many male clerks in, for example, the electrical department.

He remembered how she kept a red-cushioned stool in the fireplace instead of fires.

He remembered how she said she mostly just cried.

He remembered how she said he was the male version of Marjorie.

He remembered how her eyes went down toward her shoes when she no longer wanted to fight.

Fat American watching the hawk-haired fella zipping up his blue jacket, Morrison remembered thinking whilst crossing the plaza just before his fliering job ended for good. Morrison arrived at the top of a street and the lights had gone orange down it as far as he could see, the way they made you sad in the night, that orange, and one light way at the end of the street flickered, and Morrison moved to the first mail slot and he flipped it and flipped in a flier and he seemed to see an eye in the house behind the slot, a single disembodied eye watching out at him, and Morrison thought of his own eye looking back, and he thought of the two eyes of him as though he were outside himself looking at his two eyes looking, and he thought of the single eye of the Other on the other side of the mailslot not making contact with his own eyes. He shook himself all over and moved to the next mailslot and flicked it and chucked in a flier, and he caught a glimpse for certain this time of just one disembodied eye beyond the mailslot watching out at him. *What's with this street and everyone waiting for me behind their doors?* he thought, and carried on, and flipped the next mailslot at the next house and shoved a flier through and in dim green light, through said mailslot, he could see just simply one more disembodied eye, watching out at him watching out at him watching out at him, and he hurried on, wondering why these watching waiting eyes didn't belong to people who emerged from their houses to scold him for fliering, but no one emerged. Maybe they liked getting the fliers. He went to a fourth house, and there indeed another disembodied eye could be seen, making eye contact with Morrison's own eye in the momentary glimpse through the door that the flick of the mailslot's own door allowed. *Have I finally fliered too much, fliered every possible house in this city, and now they've conspired and are awaiting me and if so, why? They only seem to be watching, they don't emerge and pounce on my back as I hurry back down each walk...*

The fifth door was different. The mailslot was lower and Morrison couldn't see through without hunching. He slid in a flier though, sticking his fingers well into the slot, and a yowl sounded from the far side of the door and he felt a sizeable talon rend his index finger. A hot sort of pain, and

Morrison jerked his fingers out of the slot. The yowl shifted to a growl. Morrison looked at his index finger. The top knuckle was sliced wide and splayed. Like a top-joint-of-the-index-finger-sized-fish filleted. "Ow," said Morrison, and with blood pouring, he lifted the flap again, but only with the index finger's fingernail, and he crouched and peered through. The creature was in the entryway beyond, lit rose and prancing with territorial anger, its gills vented, its back up, its silver fur up, its scaled tail tip carving a million quick small circles. Morrison let down the flap. He watched his finger drip. It would surely need stitches.

Morrison decided to quit the fliering job right then, in that moment. The hours were bad and the walks were always dangerous in various ways. In fact, the only positive slice of the job Morrison could think of was Pike and his mystery van, but Morrison was accustomed to that mystery now, and would soon even grow bored of it. He dumped the rest of the fliers into a nearby recycling bin. The next day he didn't go out to meet Pike and the van. Pike had once said, "If you don't come out to meet me even once I'll assume you're quitting and I'll never show up again." True to his word, Ol' Pike, it turned out.

Morrison soon got a day job, stuffing envelopes. It was a wisp of a job but it tired him. He would fall asleep in the early evenings with the television running and he would sleep unstoppably, unceasingly, until no matter what channel would go off air in the wee hours, the giant would come and stick its eye to the other side of the television screen and watch poor Morrison through a veil of static.

- The End -

Aurora

Momma always said: *Please don't lick the train, Aurora. Very dirty.*

And when Aurora kissed Stanley with a mouthful of blood she thought as a sidebar thought that maybe world affairs being what they were people should just cut the crap and start filling their gas tanks with blood.

Or Aurora would stuff her mouth full of marbles and let them drip out one by one.

Both his thumbnails grown longer than acceptable was always what put Aurora off her food, but never kept her own fingernails from her own teeth, in the vicinity of Naylor. Naylor's girlfriend had a name Aurora could never remember and the girlfriend had such a bad hunch to her shoulders. So Aurora never got to know Naylor very well and couldn't summon up anything more than a lipped O of surprise when she heard Naylor and his girlfriend died in a car crash.

After her first kiss, Aurora walked in clouds across the same school dance floor her great-grandfather had done a dance marathon on eighty years earlier. Her great-grand-father jabbered about as much ad nauseum. He said he was extremely lucky not to have died so that therefore Aurora could live.

Or Aurora would hover over sandwiches like a dog playing beg. She would sit in her prayer chair talking to her creature teachers.

Her tears fell everywhere all over her lap or anyway those she couldn't catch in her mouth for the fine taste of salt or she thought about how they'd stick seven different kinds of needles in her skull to get rid of her oral fixation.

"Spit through the gate and a ghost will come over the

hill with two lanterns to see who you are," he said to Aurora.

Note to self to do such-and-such, she thinks, before thinking: *Note to self to brush teeth.*

Just because your nose is there to pick doesn't mean you pick it and just because a war is there to fight doesn't mean you fight it and just because you can smoke and like it doesn't mean you smoke, she thought.

She stood looking in the mirror, talking to her girlfriend next to her via its sparkling surface.

In her dying days Aurora was the woman who always brought her blanket to a bus stop and nervously gnawed a hank of its fabric.

- The End -

At Roundfire we publish great stories. We lean towards the spiritual and thought-provoking. But whether it's literary or popular, a gentle tale or a pulsating thriller, the connecting theme in all Roundfire fiction titles is that once you pick them up you won't want to put them down.